"In exquisite prose, Maud Casey has built a city inside a book, a city that is a hospital, a museum, a dance, a body in ecstasy just outside the frame. On every page of this achingly beautiful book, Casey brings a wise and feral attention to the so-called incurables of the 'era of soul science'—Augustine, Louise, Marie, Geneviève, and a chorus of nameless others singing their private beginnings and public ends."
—**Danielle Dutton**, author of *SPRAWL* and *Margaret the First*

Select Praise for Maud Casey

"Casey is a consummate stylist. . . . This is a writer who pays deep, sensual attention to the world."
—**Geraldine Brooks,** *New York Times Book Review*

"Brilliant."
—**Lauren Groff**, author of *Fates and Furies* and *Florida*

"Wildly original."
—**Joan Silber**, author of *Ideas of Heaven* and *Improvement*

"[A] compassionate, joyful, lyrical voice."
—**George Saunders**, author of *Lincoln In the Bardo* and *Fox 8*

"Deeply empathetic and rigorously intelligent."
—**Alice Sebold**, author of *The Lovely Bones* and *The Almost Moon*

"A rich and wonderfully unpredictable talent."
—**John Searles**, author of *Strange But True* and *Help for the Haunted*

"Casey writes so evocatively about family love, loss, and madness that she can break your heart."
—**Julia Glass**, author of *Three Junes* and *A House Among the Trees*

"Like Eudora Welty, Maud Casey aims her considerable art at such nearly unsayable recognitions."
—**Stuart Dybek**, author of *The Coast of Chicago* and *Paper Lantern*

"Casey writes the way Elizabeth Bowen might if she lived here, and now."
—**Andrea Barrett**, author of *Ship Fever* and *Archangel*

"*Listen.* It's a command that Maud Casey's quick to utter. . . . With good reason: If you're listening closely enough, you might just hear her pull off a feat as graceful as it is clever. Out of the clanging of church bells, the ticking of watches, the snatches of overheard phrases . . . out of this hectic mess of sounds, she manages to create a delicate harmony."
—**NPR**

"Casey evokes—with no shortage of verve and gusto—the romance of 19th-century Europe, when madness plagued more than asylums . . . bringing each internee, each insanity alive with such tenderness."
—*Washington Post*

"A sensitive and courageous chronicler. . . . [Casey's lines] absolutely soar with illuminating little details that crack everything open and reach for hope."
—*Hartford Courant*

"[Casey] shows us not just the origins of psychological conditions, but the language to describe them as well."
—*Rumpus*

CITY
—OF—
INCURABLE WOMEN

Maud Casey

Bellevue Literary Press
New York

First published in the United States in 2022
by Bellevue Literary Press, New York

For information, contact:
Bellevue Literary Press
90 Broad Street
Suite 2100
New York, NY 10004
www.blpress.org

This is a work of fiction. Characters, organizations, events, and
places (even those that are actual) are either products of the author's
imagination or are used fictitiously.

A list of publications where certain chapters in this novel first appeared is on page
126 and constitutes an extension of this copyright page.

Library of Congress Cataloging-in-Publication Data
Names: Casey, Maud, author.
Title: City of incurable women / Maud Casey.
Description: First edition. | New York : Bellevue Literary Press, 2022. |
Includes bibliographical references.
Identifiers: LCCN 2021001708 | ISBN 9781942658863 (paperback) |
ISBN   9781942658900 (epub)
Subjects: LCSH: Women patients--France--History--19th century. |
Psychiatric hospital patients--France--History--19th century. |
Salpêtrière (Hospital)
Classification: LCC PS3553.A79338 C58 2021 | DDC 814/.6--dc23
LC record available at https://lccn.loc.gov/2021001708

Bellevue Literary Press would like to thank all its generous
donors—individuals and foundations—for their support.

 This publication is made possible by the New York
State Council on the Arts with the support of the Office
of the Governor and the New York State Legislature.

Book design and composition by Mulberry Tree Press, Inc.

Bellevue Literary Press is committed to ecological stewardship
in our book production practices, working to reduce our impact
on the natural environment.

∞ This book is printed on acid-free paper.

Manufactured in the United States of America.

First Edition

3   5   7   9   8   6   4   2

paperback ISBN: 978-1-942658-86-3

ebook ISBN: 978-1-942658-90-0

For my fellow incurables

[Her] body obeys no law other than the law of the strange and the impossible.

—Paul Richer
Etudes cliniques sur la grande hystérie
ou hystéro-épilepsie (1885)

Contents

Prologue   11

The City Itself   15

Twenty Thousand Leagues Under the Sea   24

In the Before   33

The Dull Stage of Reality   42

Time's Signature   47

The Inclination to Believe   51

Her Godly Imagination   61

Father, Ether, Sea   72

Never the Same Way Twice   90

The Bells of Loudun   99

Whipping Nettles   106

A Heartless Child   109

Bodies, We Are in Them   119

Notes and Credits   122

Acknowledgments   127

The hospital has always been a museum full of dead things. Anatomical drawings. A cabinet full of skulls and spinal columns. Entire skeletons. Plaster casts of our bodies. Endless photographs of us—this girl making this shape, that girl making another, clenched toes, a hand cupping the dark. Are the photographs dead, too? I float outside the frame, not dead at all. It is true there are things I would prefer not to discuss. For example, all the things you want to know. The spells and lethargic states? I could not do otherwise. Besides, it was not a bit of fun. Simulation? Lots of fakes tried; the great doctor gave them one look and said, Be still. I float outside the frame, not still at all. What difference does it make? I lie all day long, here where there are no days. I was born to go nowhere, but I am everywhere, the child of the sounding sea, that glittering vision of the infinite, always and forever offering itself up. I offer myself up. I would say the sea was generous, that I was, but that is beside the point. I am beside the point, right beside it. I am not abandoned, only unfortunate, and some days I am not even unfortunate. Other days, I just float. Once, for example, in a long-gone winter not gone at all, I stood on a jetty. The rain fell on the surface of the ocean, and that was all.

The City Itself

The great asylum, as you are all surely aware, contains a population of over 5,000 people, including a great number called incurables who are admitted for life. ... In other words, we are in possession of a kind of living pathological museum, the resources of which are considerable.

—JEAN-MARTIN CHARCOT
Leçons sur les maladies du système nerveux,
Oeuvres Complètes, vol. 3 (1886–1893)

THE CITY IS, IN MANY WAYS, like other cities. Like other cities, it was built alongside a river and has a series of low, rambling buildings, at the center of which is the domed chapel of a cruciform church. In the chapel, Chapelle Saint-Louis, the great doctor will one day lie in state. We will be invited to pass through, to look upon his dead face; those of us who can't walk will be brought on stretchers. From a stretcher, it will be harder to look upon his dead face, but they will tell us that to see his face is not the point, though we will have had enough of the point by then because we have had enough of the point already. Not pointed at all, but dull and dusty, left somewhere on the side of the road as we were walking to where who can even remember. Still, who wouldn't look? We will look as he looked, seeking out the disease. Did you leave this world gently, our mothers' and fathers' wish until it wasn't, because they could not find gentleness in the world, and so why would leaving be any different? Anyway, who leaves this world gently? We will look the way we all look when studying a face that has studied us. Who are you who am I where are we going what is this feeling inside of me why why why what does it all mean, etc.

His last words? *I am feeling a little better.*

How about now?

As in other cities, there are alleys with pollarded plane trees, which, if you know the way, will take you the back route to the market, the bakery, the laundry, the vegetable gardens, the school where we learn grammar, history, geography, and sums, the gymnasium where we learn to bend and not to break, the library where those of us who are able to read borrow books about other cities, the post office where those of us who are able to write consider posting the letters we might someday write; until then, we write in our head or trace them in the dark on one another's backs. We take a back-alley route to the cemetery, where sometimes we go to visit ourselves. In other words, as in other cities, there are places to live and places to die.

In the city, we are dimly aware of the other cities, the villages, the farms, where we were born or found, or we found ourselves, places we left behind as this city wrapped itself around us like time. Until it became the only city. The places from the before fade, grow fainter, farther away, until it is too far to travel even in our minds. For example, the city that contains our city? The one outside the wrought-iron gates, which open onto, where else, le boulevard de l'Hôpital? We can't be sure we didn't make it up altogether.

The city is, in other ways, unlike other cities. In the courtyard, sometimes there are masked balls where famous scientists and artists and doctors dress as robed monks, musketeers, knights in armor. On those nights, the great pavilion is strung with fairy lamps, colored lanterns, flowers, and streamers, and we dance as though we are Jane Avril at the Moulin Rouge and then, look, there is Jane Avril. No, really. There she is, a citizen of the city, too, for a brief while. *The luxurious pain of a body in the throes of its symptoms* has been likened to a dance, and when she, a dancer, was a body in pain, it was something to behold.

Unlike other cities, there is a photography annex with platforms that fill an entire studio, platforms along whose length we walk because the way we walk is worth capturing and inscribing on plates of glass. There are headrests for close range, large-scale photographs of our heads or parts of our faces—our eyes, our mouths, our noses, our ears. Longer exposure requires immobility, and so iron gallows to suspend those of us who can't walk or hold ourselves upright, those of us who will eventually be carried on stretchers, those of us who will be told it is not the point to see the great doctor's dead face when he lies in state, at which point we will wonder, as we sometimes do when we are poked or pinched by some suspension apparatus, why does everything have to be so pointed?

The city, like other cities, has a history. The city, for example, began as an arsenal. As with other cities, its history is contained in its name: Salpêtrière. In Latin, *sal petrae*. Salt of stone. Saltpeter. Sparkling white crystals that grow on stone walls and hardened soil and other damp, dark places—trash pits, dovecots, henhouses, barnyards, cellars, and crypts. Sparkling white crystals, which, when mixed with other things, it is eventually discovered, are an essential ingredient for gunpowder.

In the before, we were daughters, daughters of all sorts of people who themselves were the sons and daughters of all sorts of people, and so on. Sometimes an *I* breaks free and one of us was the granddaughter of a peterman, whose job it was to scrape off, dig out, unearth the white salt crystals wherever he found them, ripping up privies and the floors of houses. When demand was high, Grandfather collected piss, which, when filtered, yields the same sparkling white crystals as cling to stone. Why not? Our bodies, my body, as damp as dark as any other damp, dark place; damper, darker. Grandfather's curiosity about the history of his trade grew from having to defend himself to those whose privies and homes he ripped up. He wanted, as most of us do, to convince himself there was meaning in his days beyond destruction and filtered piss crystals.

Curiosity means we know, too, the story of the alchemist in ancient China looking for a cure for mortality. What wouldn't any one of us do to keep death as distant as the city outside the wrought-iron gates? If we can imagine it, we'll do it, and we are renowned for our imaginations. None of us is foolish or inexhaustible or unimaginative enough to want to ward death off forever. Only an emperor would ask for the cure. His gilded life, why wouldn't he? Fix it, this emperor said to the alchemist, who, having dealt with emperors before, got immediately to work, no questions asked. He ground sulfur into a fine powder, added honey, waited as long as he dared to be inspired. Finally, one night, as he walked through the graveyard, his own version of staving off mortality, there, on the gravestones, the white crystal sparkling. When he heated the mixture with the sulfur and the honey, sure enough: flames and a cloud of smoke. Even if it failed to cure the emperor's mortality, the pyrotechnics would impress him; anyway, if it failed to cure his mortality, he would be dead. The fire drug, the alchemist called it, and it became famous. Impervious to the roughest handling, it slowed the decomposition of the hulls of the ships that carried it from China to India to the Middle East and eventually to Europe, where it began its career as gunpowder, that crucial ingredient in the engine of empire. Bengal saltpeter, one of the reasons Napoléon was keen to wrest India from the English.

Enough, we say to Grandfather, tired of his lectures.

His last words? *Pass the salt.* Of course those weren't his last words. There are some things whose value increases for having never been recorded, by virtue of being kept private. Privacy makes history around here. Privacy, like history, is something worth imagining. What, we wonder, would our grandfather think of this city of incurables built of saltpeter?

In the before, we were all kinds of girls. A daughter, for example, who missed 150 days of school because of bad reading habits, which, according to the *Report on the Service of the Insane of the Department of the Seine in the Year 1877,* is one of the twenty-one moral causes of death, alongside nostalgia, misery, love, and joy. In the before, we read *Natural Magic,* by Giambattista della Porta, Italian scholar and polymath, friend of the German astronomer Johannes Kepler, and Galileo, jailed by the Inquisition for what the Church considered to be his heretical pursuits, none of which included the invention of gunpowder. In della Porta's magic book of secrets, he described a mighty cold produced by a mixture of saltpeter and snow. Our grandfather the saltpeter man knew that the ancient Greeks and Romans had thought to use it not only for heat but for cold; he knew, too, that, because of the fall of the

Roman Empire, the knowledge of saltpeter's cooling proper-
ties was lost until several Arabic manuscripts were translated
into European languages and the knowledge reappeared, as
knowledge often does, as if it were being discovered for the first
time. We girls with bad reading habits read of saltpeter's magic
as if we were discovering it, the way reading makes you feel as
though the gunpowder words have been waiting all this time
for you, only you, to light them on fire. We read of saltpeter's
use as an ingredient in love or money spells. In order to shield
yourself where you walk, sprinkle some in your shoe; in order
to ward off jinxes and protect from attack, take a protective
saltpeter bath or, better yet, prepare a floor wash out of saltpeter and urine. Do this in complete silence. Mop from the
doorway outward in order to ward off evil. We girls with bad
reading habits read of saltpeter's magic as a curative for the
mild headache, the upset stomach, kidney damage, an antidote
to the male libido. We who live in the city of saltpeter have our
theories about the unlikelihood of this last curative.

   We are in the city and the city is in us. We are the traces of
saltpeter left over from the city's days as an arsenal, lurking in
straw beds in the basement cells, in the cracks of the courtyard
stones. We are the stray particles in the air when the arsenal
became a public hospital for destitute women and prostitutes,
then a women's prison, then the largest asylum in Europe, then
the largest brothel. We are the dust the revolutionary mob
stirred up when it stormed the wrought-iron gates, streaming
in from le boulevard de l'Hôpital to free the prostitutes. When
Pinel, the great humanitarian reformer, unchained the women
shackled in the courtyard for public display, we rose up from
the straw beds set on fire and clung to the building's stone. A
painting celebrating his triumph hangs in the foyer of the main

hospital in the city. He stands solemnly, having just broken the chains of the bare-breasted woman standing next to him. Her arm extended, she examines it, this object suddenly unbound but not yet an arm. Is it hers? The painting knows it is often too late to triumph over terror. If you look in the direction she is looking, there we are, we are there still, sparkling on the stones of the building that became the city itself. Someday our grandfather will come looking for us. He will scrape us off the walls; dig us out of the floorboards; sift us out of the piss in the privies. He will gather us to him.

Our last words? We are still considering. We'll let you know.

Sometimes the pollarded plane trees cast unexpected morning shadows. We, the posthumous daughters and granddaughters and so on and whatnot, shortcutting our way to the market or the library or the cemetery, have only to look at one another. Do you see it there? The city inside the city, the shadow city? Would you like to go with me? Our eyes ask the questions only for the pleasure of asking and being asked. We are there already. It is where we live.

Photographic Service
Voucher for the photograph of M. Gleizes

Room: Dûchenne
Age: 17
Previous Residence:
L'Hôpital des Enfants-Malades

Photograph nos: 1510, 1511, 1512
Stereoscope

Projection
Proofs: two on each side

Diagnosis
Hysteria, bouts of rhythmic chorea

Information
Present since patient's arrival (two years).
At onset of attack, patient gapes, cries out.

23 October 1877

LE CINQUANTENAIRE DE L'HYSTERIE

(1878-1928)

Nous, surréalistes, tenons a célébrer ici le cinquantenaire de l'hystérie, la plus grande découverte poétique de la fin du XIXe siècle, et cela au moment même où le démembrement du concept de l'hystérie paraît chose consommée. Nous qui n'aimons rien tant que ces jeunes hystériques, dont le type parfait nous est fourni par l'observation relative a la délicieuse X. L. (Augustine) entrée a la Salpétrière dans le service du Dr Charcot le 21 octobre 1875, a l'age de 15 ans 1/2, comment serions-nous touchés par la laborieuse réfutation de troubles organiques, dont le procès ne sera jamais qu'aux yeux des seuls médecins celui de l'hystérie ? Quelle pitié ! M. Babinski, l'homme le plus intelligent qui se soit attaqué a cette question, osait publier en 1913 : « Quand une émotion est sincère, profonde, secoue l'ame humaine, il n'y a plus de place pour l'hystérie ». Et voila encore ce qu'on nous a donné a apprendre de mieux. Freud, qui doit tant a Charcot, se souvient-il du temps où, au témoignage des survivants, les internes de la Salpétrière confondaient leur devoir professionnel et leur gout de l'amour, où, a la nuit tombante, les malades les rejoignaient au dehors ou les recevaient dans leur lit ? Ils énuméraient ensuite patiemment, pour les besoins de la cause médicale qui ne se défend pas, les attitudes passionnelles soi-disant pathologiques qui leur étaient, et nous sont encore humainement, si précieuses. Après cinquante ans, l'école de Nancy est-elle morte ? S'il vit toujours, le docteur Luys a-t-il oublié ? Mais où sont les observations de Néri sur le tremblement de terre de Messine ? Où sont les zouaves torpillés par le Raymond Roussel de la science, Clovis Vincent?

Aux diverses définitions de l'hystérie qui ont été données jusqu'a ce jour, de l'hystérie, divine dans l'antiquité, infernale au Moyen-Age, des possédés de Loudun aux flagellants de N.-D. des Pleurs (vive Madame Chantelouve!), définitions mythiques, érotiques ou simplement lyriques, définitions sociales, définitions savantes, il est trop facile d'opposer cette « maladie complexe et protéiforme appelée hystérie qui échappe a toute définition » (Bernheim). Les spectateurs du très beau film « La Sorcellerie a travers les ages » se rappellent certainement avoir trouvé sur l'écran ou dans la salle des enseignements plus vifs que ceux des livres d'Hippocrate, de Platon où l'utérus bondit comme une petite chèvre, de Galien qui immobilise la chèvre, de Fernel qui la remet en marche au XVIe siècle et la sent sous sa main remonter jusqu'a l'estomac; ils ont vu grandir, grandir les cornes de la

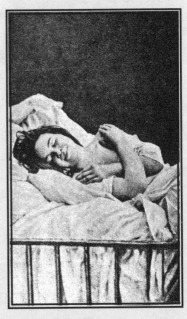

LES ATTITUDES PASSIONNELLES EN 1878

Twenty Thousand Leagues
Under the Sea

We, Surrealists, insist on celebrating here [in 1928] the
fiftieth anniversary of hysteria, the greatest poetic discovery
of the end of the nineteenth century . . .

ANDRÉ BRETON AND LOUIS ARAGON's homage to the
anniversary of the diagnosis in *La Révolution surréaliste* is accompanied by reproductions of the original series of
photographs, titled *Passionate Attitudes, 1878*. Plate 1, *The
Call*: propped on an elbow, thick hair hanging down her back.
Plate 2, *Eroticism*: arms hugged to her chest, as though she is
sleeping. Plate 3, *Contracture*: Head tilted, lips pursed, she
sits up in bed wearing only a sheet. Follow the slope of her
bare shoulder down her arm to find the paralysis, clenched
fist camouflaged in bunched bedding. Plate 4, *Mockery*: She
tsks someone no one else can see. Plate 5, *The Cry*: tongue
stuck out of a twisted face.

Her clever escape from the Salpêtrière dressed as a man
has always been the end of the story, but lives have a way of
exceeding their narratives.

Her saints' days belonged to men. May 26 and August
28, Saint Augustine, Apostle of England, and Saint Augustine of Tagaste, in Algeria. Saint Augustine from England
was the prior of the monastery of Saint Andrew and founded

the Anglo-Saxon church. St. Augustine from Tagaste ended up in Milan, full of doubt, then found his way to a secret garden, where he heard a voice. *Take and read.* Take what? Read what? The nuns at the convent school disliked it when she asked questions. Whatever it was he took, he read in it *walk honestly as in the day* and understood it to mean get baptized and give everything to the poor, which he did; then he became a bishop and settled at Hippo. She'd grown bored by the *Lives of the Saints*, its guiding hand forever moving her toward a moral. The reflection at the end of each entry could be boiled down: Poverty is good, suffering and death better, submit, submit, submit. There was much talk of the odor of sanctity, and though she didn't know exactly what that smelled like, she knew an *odor* never smelled good. Sanctity, even worse.

January 1, dedicated to the circumcision of our Lord. Why? *Shh,* Augustine. *Listen. Wait until we sing. When you sing, you pray twice. Saint Augustine said that.* September 30, Jerome, the lone doctor, born in Dalmatia in 329, sent to Rome for school, devoted himself to science, but Christ needed him, so he fled to the Syrian Desert to be in solitude. Solitude, why was it so great? The nuns didn't even look up from the lesson. Jerome prayed and received divine wisdom. The Pope asked him to revise the Latin Bible with the wisdom he received, after which he became a hermit. Everyone was forever becoming a hermit.

Teresa's heart was pierced with divine love? That she could understand. She could feel the story about to begin. She could feel the whole of Teresa's life, a vibration, beginning to end. One day, years from then, Augustine would dress as the male version of herself, slip out the back of the hospital, escape, her own heart pierced by something she couldn't name. She would feel herself about to begin.

> *We who love nothing so much as those young hysterics, the perfect example of whom is supplied to us by the study concerning the delicious Augustine—admitted to the Salpêtrière in Dr. Charcot's care. 21 October 1875, at the age of fifteen and a half.*

Was she still delicious, fifty years later? Oh yes. The man on the street was handing the journals out to everyone who passed, but she likes to think her deliciousness is why, as he put one directly into her hands, his lingered.

"You cannot claim to have really seen something until it is photographed," the great doctor said to the men gathered around her in the amphitheater. "Listen to the photographs. They will tell you all you need to know."

Shh. Listen.

Fifty years later, she'd rather be reading the novel given to her by a lover. You've wondered? She's had many lovers. Since her escape in clothes stolen from an intern, she has come to understand that the infection the doctor said came from an invisible lesion on her brain cannot be yanked out. Sex with her most recent lover was like breathing underwater, she told him, and he gave her a novel about a sea expedition in search of a mysterious sea monster, which eventually turns out to be a submarine. She was charmed. Anyway, she likes a sea adventure.

It's hard to hear at first what the photographs are saying across the years, but, like her image on the plates, it begins, slowly, to take shape.

In each photograph, a girl in a bed against a black

backdrop. The doctor was an eye-twister; he twisted her eyes. Still, there is the girl in a bed in a night that was the world.

When she arrived in the amphitheater, she would shake the braids out of her hair as if she were shaking everyone out of the room. Sometimes she was a magnet and all the men little pieces of metal waiting to be drawn up. When she arrived, the air, hot and thick, shimmered with electricity.

"The neurologic tree has many branches," the great doctor said, pointing at her clenched fist. "Each has a different fruit."

"One thinks one has dreamed something," she said. Some days, she knew exactly what to say. She looked straight into the fruit of the great doctor's brain. Some days, the words came as if in a dream. "But it wasn't a dream at all."

"And now," the great doctor said to the audience, "I will give you firsthand experience of this pain."

"Get rid of the snake in your pants," she said.

She performed an idea of sex, writhing on the floor. It gave the endless ache she couldn't name shape where there was no shape; it gave it a name when there was no name. For a moment, it explained everything. The men in the amphitheater clapped. When the doctor reached inside to adjust her, it pleased her to know the seed of her pain was nowhere he would find it. After, it was nowhere she could find it, either. No shape, no name, the ache went on and on.

Once upon a time, she had two gangly brothers. They wrestled constantly. Their bodies, so unlike her own, fascinated her. She never eats enough, her mother would say to her father, who had recently moved the family to the city so he and the brothers could work in the textile factory that dyed their fingers blue. She is fine, her father would say. She *was* fine, rosy and plump, one of those children who brimmed with love. What a relief when her mother finally took her out of the convent school, where she was being bored to death by the *Lives of the Saints*, to work as a chambermaid in the home of Mr. C. When he threatened Augustine with a razor and threw her on the bed, it was not her brimming love he was after. When her fits began, her mother was relieved; she could send her away from that house.

In the back of the journal designed to look like a scientific journal is an ad for portraiture: "Resemblance Guaranteed." The girl in the photographs does resemble her; that face is inside her face still when she looks in the mirror.

Sweet, clever girl, she thinks, poignant to herself in plate 6, *Ecstasy*: hands reaching heavenward. Three seconds between each plate, three seconds for each pose. She learned the speed of the shutter. The photographer squeezed the stereoscopic bulb only after he framed the shot, adjusted the light. She held the pose even as the flash lit up the room; the moment that might have been lost forever, illuminated. Is this her, the girl you want? In the photographs, that girl will never die, or she will always be dead.

The doctor is long dead, his theories derided. On certain days, she misses him. It takes her by surprise. The smell of sawdust in the streets one day sent her back to the sawdust (in case there was blood) on the floor of the amphitheater. There were his eyes, so expectant, better than desire because it was something he needed from her, not something he could just take. There were days it was clear he wanted her to surprise him. Since his death, it is said *hysterics suffer primarily from reminiscences*. She reads novels to avoid reminiscing, to avoid the dream in which she grows smaller after the doctor moved her out of the private room back onto the ward of incurables. Some of the women looked like her mother, but they were never her mother, who had died, though no one told her. In the dream, she grows so small in that crowded room of almost mothers that she misplaces herself. She might be the woman in the corner there or that one there or that one there.

Once, when she was still the doctor's best girl, he left her alone in his office. Who wouldn't have looked at the papers on his desk? *Report on the Service of the Insane of the Department of the Seine in the Year 1877.* One doctor for every five hundred patients. Three different kinds of diets: two meals, one meal, and starvation. The rate of cure: 9.72 percent. According to the report, 254 women died that year of causes due to insanity. Thirty-eight physical causes, such as scrofula, blows, wounds, alcohol, debauchery, licentiousness, and masturbation; twenty-one moral causes, such as nostalgia, misery, love, joy, and bad reading habits.

"Her world is without color," the doctor had said. But there's color still.

> *We propose therefore, in 1928, a new definition of hysteria: Hysteria is a more or less irreducible mental state, characterizing itself by the subversion of the links established between the subject and the moral world, of which he believes he is indeed a part, outside of any system of madness. The mental state is founded on the need for a reciprocal seduction, which explains the hastily accepted miracles of medical suggestion. Hysteria is not a pathological phenomenon and can, in all respects, be considered as a supreme means of expression.*

She puts another log on the fire. She puts the journal on the fire. She returns to her novel about the mysterious sea creature, which eventually turns out to be the submarine. As the journal burns, the submarine takes the men around the world, twenty thousand leagues—to the Antarctic ice shelves, to the corals of the Red Sea, to Atlantis. The captain is monomaniacal, and ultimately, having abandoned his crew, he disappears into a maelstrom off the coast of Normandy. She understands Captain Nemo's desire for exile. But she is not Nemo. She is not nobody. Her favorite is the scene when the giant squid attacks one of the crew. She has read it over and over. Tonight, as often happened when she was the girl in the photographs, her mind delights her with its inventiveness.

In her own one-person submersible, she sinks into the ocean, black as the night in those pictures where she floated, but here there is no frame; the liquid world goes on forever. There, in the expansive underwater night, she meets the giant squid. It presses its eye to the window of the submersible. It looks directly at her, the way she looked into the camera. Unashamed, the doctor had said. An accusation, but admiration, too. Unashamed, the giant squid reaches out its tentacles to her. It takes the submersible in its many arms. Augustine, delicious Augustine, its giant eye says to her, the rest of life is in the sea.

Case Notes (1886):

4 January – Menstruation began. Tremors in arms and legs. Rapid swallowing. Palpitation of eyelids.

26 February – Menstruation began. Hemianesthesia on the entire right side. Paralysis on the left. Legs and arms are rigid.

4 March – Thirty-five attacks; stopped by amyl nitrate.

9 March – From eight o'clock to midnight, thirty-six attacks. Sensitivity on both sides. Vomiting, diarrhea, probably from morphine (doses of two, four, or six centigrams).

17 March – Forty-three attacks. Temporary contractures, calmed by ether.

18 March – Sixty attacks. Several inhalations of ether. Attacks stopped definitively by amyl nitrate.

20 March – Menstruation began yesterday. Fit of anger.

April – Menstruation, five attacks.

May – No menstruation, no attacks. Spasms, contractions, writhing. She gets excited whenever she is not given subcutaneous injections, ether or chloroform. Unfortunately, we give in too often.

June – No menstruation, no attacks.

July – No menstruation, thirteen attacks.

August – No menstruation, no attacks.

September – No menstruation, no attacks.

October – No menstruation, no attacks.

November – No menstruation, no attacks.

December – Since April, she has had from three to six daily injections of a solution composed of one gram morphine to thirty grams water and, often, in addition, ether and chloroform. From time to time, a julep with four grams of calomel.

Photographic Service
Voucher for the photograph of M. Dubois

Room: Leguin
Age: 20
Residence: 3, rue Cels

Photograph nos: 4259, 4260, 4261, 4262
Stereoscope
Projection
Proofs: two on each side

Diagnosis
Hysteria, contracture of the hand

Information
Present for six months.
Occurred following a violent emotion.

12 August 1890

In the Before

The female hysteric represents an extraordinarily compli-
cated type, of a completely particular and excessively versa-
tile nature, remarkable for her spirit of duplicity, lying and
simulation. With an essentially perverse nature, the hysteric seeks to fool those around her, in the same way that
she has impulses that push her to steal, to falsely accuse, to
set things on fire.

—GILLES DE LA TOURETTE
*Traité clinique et thérapeutique de l'hystérie
d'après l'enseignement de la Salpêtrière*

THE COLOR OF THE ERA OF PSYCHIATRY, that science of
the soul, is red. The red of longing, the red of sex and
fantasy sex. The red of love alleged to reside in the heart,
which, so we've been told, is also red, though who of us
has seen a heart? The color of the era of soul science is red,
though in the before we didn't yet think in eras. For a short
while, we didn't think about sex, either. Instead, we listened
for the names our mothers and fathers called us: *mon petit
chou, ma chérie, ma poulette, ma puce, ma bichette, mon bichon,
mon bout de chou, ma poupée, ma princesse.* After the short
while was over, there were the names men, some of them our
lovers, called us: *mon cœur, mon lapin, mon ange, mon amour,
mon chaton, mon loulou, ma moitié, mon doudou, ma chérie,*
and others we will never tell you. Here, those of us not yet

fluent in the language of hysteria, the language of our pain—
amorous supplications, eroticism, ecstasy, hallucinations,
crucifixion, mockery, menace, the cry, etc.—have no names.
Those who have mastered that language are the prettiest or
the most ecstatic, the doctor's best girls until another best
girl comes along. The best girls are lifted up out of the crowd
and slipped between clean sheets in a private room where
there are windows to open and close, and quiet to hear their
thoughts. We, the unfluent, the unbest, are the left-behind
crowd, a jumble of limbs, a tangle of unwashed hair, the smell
of dirt in the creases of the backs of knees, the damp rust
smell of blood when we bleed, though some of us never begin.
In other words, our indistinction distinguishes us.

Sometimes we hold hands to feel the difference between
us. *This* body, *that* body. Sometimes, those of us who can write
use our fingers to trace the names we tell no one on one another's backs, the way the doctors sometimes write on our skin
the name of what ails us, or their own names, or the name
of the hospital. Bright red lines rise to meet the metal of the
knife tracing letters on our skin. Our blood writes itself from
the inside out; the words become scars; the scars disappear.
When we trace our secret names on one another's backs, we
do not draw blood. If only we had knives. Those of us who
can't write letters trace shapes—circles or squares or ones we've
invented—that ask questions designed to bring one another
closer. Sometimes we use our mouths. Down the staircase of a
spine: Where you are from, did it smell like chicory and anise?
Over the curve of an ass: What did your mother's voice sound
like? Down one thigh: When you were a child, what was the
first thing you saw when you woke up? Up the other: What
was the last thing you saw before you went to sleep? We use our

tongues in the warm, wet folds our lovers in the before called *la chatte, la foufoune, le kiki,* or maybe there were no lovers, only men who rooted around like the doctors, as if it were a treasure chest down there, or a myth and not an everyday fact. The doctors root and root, looking for science or treasure or the Holy Grail. They don't find anything with their rough, unspecific hands. That's not true. Some days, a doctor surprises us, his fingers asking who are you where did you come from why why why. Our hands, our tongues are rough, but they are specific— what does your joy sound like, what does your childhood smell like, how does your sadness taste. Our fingers make words; our tongues repeat them. Then there are days we are too tired to muster the desire to desire.

When we arrived, the doctors told us Christ bled from His right side. Why, then, did He bleed from His left side where He hung on the cross over the door into the amphitheater? Was it a trick? Look again, they said, but there wasn't time to look again, and we weren't the best girls, so we didn't have occasion to ever walk underneath Christ bleeding from whichever side, into the amphitheater to perform the language of our pain. The proof of our illness was an invisible lesion on our brains; the language of our pain needed to be abundantly clear.

We, the unbest, may never have seen the amphitheater door again, but in the before we saw many doors. Endless doors: broken-down doors, doors we broke down, doors we crawled, walked, sashayed, were coaxed, led, dragged through. Once we walked through the door into the era of soul science, doors began shutting all around us, and then they disappeared. Those doors that led all sorts of places, where did they go? Where did it go, the land of doors? Sometimes still, in the jumbled, tangled, blurry dark, a door takes shape, a door swings open, and an *I* breaks free. Maybe that *I* lived by the coast and swam in the sounding sea. The door slams shut, sucked back into the darkness. Where did it go?

In the before, sometimes our mothers were women who walked through doors and gave birth out of wedlock, and then we were foundlings whose tendency for deviance came from our deviant mothers. *Enfants trouvées,* found children, though had we ever been lost? When you are in your own life, you are not lost at all. You are in the middle of it. Our bodies, we are in them. Our bodies, here they are, still, and we are here, still in them. In the before, sometimes we were foundlings carried through town hall doors, where we were given names—Anne, Josephine, Margaux, Pauline, Thérèse, Valerie, Virginie, Zoé, Marie, and names we have forgotten. We were named in front of whoever was on hand. A cobbler, a tailor, a candlestick maker, the mayor of such and such small town; witnesses to make our names real. Yes, she is called this. She is called that. Yes, that is *her. Her* and *her* and *her.* In the before, sometimes we were born the posthumous child of a miller and sent to a farm in rural Marçay, to a foster family who received the usual government payment of eighty-four francs per year for taking in a foundling. To protect a foundling from her innate tendency toward deviance, the family was told, put her to work until she turns eight. When we turned nine, sometimes we were deemed too old for foster care, and back we went through the doors of the foundling home. Lost and found and lost again. Sometimes we were sent back through the doors of the nunnery because the mother superior wanted more hands for the manufacturing of sheets. In the before, sometimes we were sent through the doors of a kind widow at the center of Poitiers, where we learned to sew, and then the widow, finding her widowhood unbearable, died.

Sometimes in the before, we were never lost to our parents, who were brush makers or storekeepers or grain and fodder merchants or worked in the factories or worked by the river doing laundry. We lived close to the Seine, easier to walk out the door and carry the loads of laundry, or we did not live close to the Seine, or our mothers were pretty enough or there was something else about them as alluring as prettiness, or maybe it was just that they were women. Whatever it was, the dockworkers held open another door, offering them different work than carrying loads of laundry. Sometimes we lived in an apartment above the hardware store, where all day long we listened to talk of nails and cookware. Or we lived in an apartment behind the hardware store, where the bedroom was dark and windowless and the walls of the kitchen were black from the stove, and our mothers were too tired to clean or whitewash because all day they cleaned and whitewashed someone else's kitchen walls. We slept in attic beds on poorly joined planks, the wind blowing through the roof, rattling the string of onions hung in a corner. Or we slept somewhere else entirely. In the before, maybe we lived in the city, under open gutters pouring shit into the streets. Or we lived in the country, where we strung out rope to dry our clothes; when they were too heavy, they fell into the vegetable garden and we had to start over, wash them again.

Sometimes in the before, we were girls who hated waking up, and our mothers pulled us out of bed, stood us up, sent us out the door with knitting—*twenty rows on that sock before you play*—for our walk to the school, which was too far to attend regularly. Sometimes we were the girl who put the knitting in her bag and forgot about it, distracted by the whip she brought along to crack at the branches of the walnut tree to make the nuts fall into her apron so she could eat them later when she was in the meadow grazing the cows, Bardella, the spotted one, and Sarina, the black one. When she walked through the school door, Delphine was her one friend, Louise the other, though sometimes she called Delphine Bardella and Louise Sarina, Bardella Louise and Sarina Delphine. Sometimes by accident and sometimes on purpose, because she loved the cows that much, because she loved her friends that much.

Sometimes restlessness made us naughty, or we suffered from utopian urges, which made us restless, too. Or we mostly behaved and then, because we were used to the country and running with the cows and the other girls, we got pins and needles from sitting too long. Our mothers sent us out the door with jump ropes to jump the pins and needles out, and when that didn't work, we walked around the courtyard and forgot to return to class, and the sister would bang on the window. Sometimes, for punishment, she would put us in a dark room behind a closed door. Sometimes, we were the girl who was put in the dark room, where there were several baskets of cherries, who was careful to even out the tops so no one would notice the ones she stole, who swallowed the pits. Sometimes the sister would say to our mothers, She's such a good student, if she would only sit still.

Sometimes our mothers thought it was the saint's illness that gave us pains in our legs. They would soak ivy leaves, placing a mark on each leaf to know which saint. The leaf that came out spotted after the soaking was our saint; our mothers would do a novena to that one. One leaf, Our Lady of Seven Sorrows; a second, Our Lady of the Willows; a third, Saint Jeanne.

Sometimes our mothers would make us wear violet. Were our pains cured from the syrup the doctors gave us, the novenas, or the violet-colored clothes our mothers made us wear? We didn't care, after the pains were gone, what it was that had made them go.

Sometimes our mothers would send food—sausage, eggs, potatoes—for the weeks at school when we stayed over. If we were lucky, out the door with a stack of waffles. At school, we all washed our hands and feet in the same enormous earthenware pot. Hands and feet, hands and feet, hands and feet, until the water was black. When we turned ten, it was time to learn the catechism, time for our First Communion. Some of us left school because of an infestation that destroyed the crops. Some of us took work behind the doors of the silk factory, where we listened all day to the sound of the *tavelles*, the skeins of silk winding round and round. The trick was to unreel the skein without breaking the thread. Sometimes we were the girl who wanted a clean apron, but her mother wouldn't give her one because her mother suspected her dirty aprons were the reason she didn't throw herself into the river after the sheriff took the furniture when her father could not pay the rent and she was left sleeping on boards. It was true, she didn't want to be found dead wearing a filthy apron.

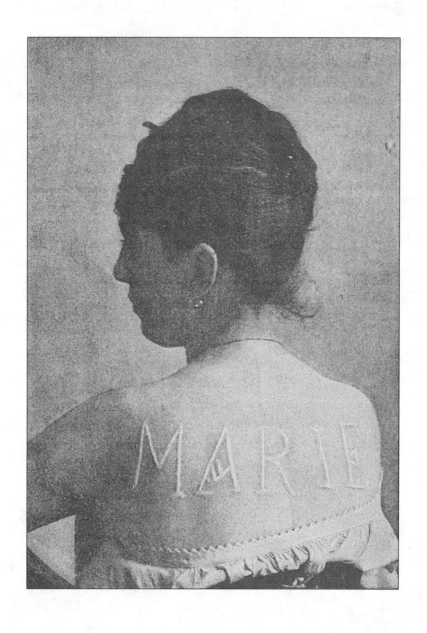

a prior fixation. This method is even convenient to use with somewhat turbulent subjects whose gaze cannot be held for long.

Fig. 4.

It is also advantageous to combine the two methods: You fix the patient's eyes by resting your thumbs on her eyebrows, the other fingers encircling her temples. It results in a kind of

The Dull Stage of Reality

Although at first an inert, plastic mass of flesh and bones
. . . the cataleptic subject allows herself to be molded at
the will of her operator. She becomes a soft wax figure on
which the most fantastic emotions can be imprinted, she
is an automaton capable of being animated.

—Dr. Foveau de Cormelles
L'Hypnotisme (1890)

THE COLOR OF THE ERA OF SOUL SCIENCE IS RED. The red
of murder. The doctors wanted us to kill them, endlessly,
in a million different ways for a million different reasons. Here
is a pistol, here is a vial of poison, here is a bludgeon. Pull the
trigger, offer the vial, swing the bludgeon. Here is a man who
has disgraced you; here, a man who has caused a falling-out
with your family; here is a man who has abandoned you and
left you all alone, more alone than you have ever been or ever
will be, they say, then gather around us groups of men. Doctors, journalists, photographers. Murder, poison, bludgeon?
Yes, of course. Our murders become famous. Before we pull
the trigger, offer the vial, raise the bludgeon, whichever man
they pointed to will ask for a kiss. Just one kiss. They like a
little cat and mouse. The man thinks he is the cat, but he would
be wrong. After the murder, men who play the role of magis-
trates are called in to deliver imaginary justice. They wake us

from our trances, *What actresses! As successful with comedy as with tragedy on the dull stage of reality.* We understand the competition, but what is the prize?

When they hypnotize us, ammonia becomes rose water, charcoal becomes chocolate, a top hat becomes a baby to be cradled. We drink, we eat, we rock our long-lost babies from the before. Their questions are never to do with the before. What before? What is the question? We are never sure, only that they have one and they have an answer, too. To be hypnotizable is proof of the invisible lesion on our brains and so proof of our hysteria.

In the before, when we were daughters of all sorts of people who themselves were the sons and daughters of all sorts of people, people who had crawled through doors—broken doors, doors they broke down, and so on and whatnot—there was no proof of anything.

In the before, sometimes our parents sent us off to be domestics. They hoped for us, their children, that we might be the faithful, not the fallen, kind. The faithful kind put away savings for a dowry, made a good prospect for a shopkeeper or an artisan, received a pension. If we were no prospect for a shopkeeper or an artisan, maybe we would make another kind of good prospect, a *grisette*, provide company for a student come to the city from the provinces. They never hoped, at least not out loud, that we would make our way to the Lorette quarter of Notre Dame and become a *lorette*, someone's pleasure in return for this or that gift, usually a meal or money. Our parents hoped for the dowry, the shopkeeper or the artisan, the pension, but what is hope if not desire and trust? Who can afford that? Hope was a luxury our parents afforded themselves, a luxury they could not afford, and still. They hoped so that we might begin with hope. We hoped to be faithful, not fallen. Who sets out to be fallen? None of us wanted to fall, but then we were falling.

Our parents knew that no matter our age, no matter whether we were faithful or fallen or faithfully fallen, we would be counted as minors, treated legally as such, and when we died, no matter who counted us or how, our bodies would be unclaimed, our graves unmarked, occasionally watery. Our mothers, who did laundry by the Seine, and we, who worked alongside our mothers, had seen bodies like ours floating by. *Femme isolée* meant both a prostitute and an independent seamstress. The confusion deliberate; there was no confusion. We would never be free, especially if we were free.

In the just before, sometimes a Monsieur B. or a Monsieur L. or a Monsieur X., Messieurs A–Z, requested us in their homes for our young, strong girl bodies. A gaggle, a charm, a flock, a plump, a wedge, a team, a pride, a gulp, a tittering, a tribe of young, strong girl bodies slipping through those doors. A city of girls, a city of doors. We were dragged, shoved, pushed through bedroom doors into the beds we made with the sheets we washed in the homes of Monsieur B. or G. or L., Messieurs A–Z. Dragged, shoved, pushed by the man of the house, whose wife hated us more than he did, especially if there was an unwanted pregnancy. Who wants an unwanted pregnancy? Back out through the doors we went—dragged, pushed, shoved.

In the just before, we lay on beds for hours, as if nailed to the cross; or we had sex with Jesus; or we were paralyzed from the waist down; or we bounced off walls in our mania until the factory owners or the nuns or our mothers and fathers were obliged to tie us up; or, when we could not find a razor or scissors to make ourselves bleed, we used our teeth; or we touched ourselves in public and laughed because it felt good and because it was outrageous. There were so many ways we didn't make sense.

Sometimes when the doctors hypnotize us, they don't want us to kill them endlessly. Sometimes they want other things. Sometimes they want what Messieurs A–Z wanted but disguise it as science. Kiss the bust of a famous dead doctor, kiss the hospital priest, kiss the wax model of one of the women just like you. Undress and take a bath in this bucket that is a bathtub. Again, we understand the competition, but what is the prize? Sometimes it is an ill-lit corner of the before, suddenly alight. Sometimes we are the hypnotized girl down the middle of whose body they draw a precise median line, a border, her body two nations, each with its own doctor playing the role of its husband caressing, careful to caress his side of the border, his nation. A *mariage à trois*, they call it, and she tries and tries to send herself into the before and then there she is, a cuckoo's call the first sound in spring when she wakes, before the church bells, before her father died and her mother sent her to the city to be a seamstress. Everyone is alive, cuckoo, cuckoo. She is quite modest, but look, look how she receives this with pleasure, a third doctor observing the caressing husbands says, and the bird cuckoos and the river rushes fierce as rain and it is morning, the day just beginning, and she is just beginning, the bird calling her down to the river's edge, where she dips her hand in the shocking cold water, and the light wanders over her, wanders over the water, but when a set of hands wanders across the line, she slaps the face to whom the hand belongs.

And you thought she wasn't paying attention, the slapped face says. She removes her blouse, leaving her corset. Let them wander that cage; let her get back to the water, but then one set of hands unlaces the corset. When she wakes up in an armchair, her corset is gone. The bird, too.

Smell the ammonia rose water, eat the charcoal chocolate. Rock your baby, the doctors said. Tenderly we rocked our longlost babies; when we woke up, they were top hats.

Time's Signature

The walls, and even the ceilings, were decorated with anatomy drawings, paintings, etchings and photographs depicting patients alone or in groups, naked or dressed, seated, lying down or standing. Sometimes the images depicted one or two legs, a hand, a torso or another body part.

—JOSEPH DELBOEUF
"Une visite à la Salpêtrière," 1886

THE COLOR OF THE ERA OF SOUL SCIENCE IS RED, the red of the desire to look and the desire to measure. The distance between the desire to look and the desire to measure? Immeasurable. The photography annex of the hospital in Paris is grand: the glass-walled studio, the dark and light laboratories, platforms, beds, screens, backdrops in all colors, headrests for those of us who cannot sit still, gallows from which to suspend those of us unable to walk or those of us who cannot be trusted to hold ourselves upright. At the end of the day, the gallows fold up tidily along the wall of the studio.

How to get the best proof? With the wet collodion plates, the trick is to avoid the darkening, we hear the photographers say, mostly to themselves, underneath their tents. Their calibrations, endless. They, we, are always waiting for the light. Everyone, at the mercy of the light or the lack of it. Only after the photographer has situated the plate, framed the shot, adjusted the lens and the distance, adjusted us, focused and focused and focused once more does he squeeze the bulb. And then, more waiting. The pictures appear slowly, chasing the movement of the illness on our bodies, capturing it, and stilling it.

In the room Duchenne, the room Bouvier, the room Requin, the room Leguin, the room Rayer, the passage Lepic, the room Cruvellier, and the room Pruss, photographs of our bodies on the platforms like a stage set. Photographs taken when we first arrived (here, someone) and the ones taken after (here, what she became). Photographs of the doctor's best girls making shapes that spell hysteria (*arc en cercle*, ecstasy or some other passionate attitude) hang in the hospital corridors, in the passageways that lead to the photography annex, to the school, where we learn grammar, history, geography, and sums, to the gymnasium, where we learn to bend and not to break, to the library, where those of us who are able to read borrow books; in the amphitheater, where those best girls make the shapes; in the offices of the doctors who teach the best girls how to make the shapes. When we first arrived, we did not know how to write the illness with the jumble of our bodies. We, the unbest girls, never learn.

We only imagine the photographs taken when we first arrived, because those photographs do not hang on the walls. A fist punching out of a frayed cuff, a thumb extended, wrinkles underlining the knuckle; a hand resting on a cloth-draped cone; a set of legs dangling from a table, one foot bent at a peculiar angle; a body in profile, its arm twisted behind its back, the spine's knobby staircase, upon which rests the hand of a doctor. Around his wrist, a watch frozen in its ticking.

We hear the photographers say the best girls know how long it takes for the photographer to capture them on the plate, to make a likeness of their illness from the magic of light; the best girls, they say, know how long to hold a pose. One of the best girls, we hear, had 1,293 attacks in one year. Convulsions, fogged vision, knots, throbbing ovaries, a globe in her throat. It is no ordinary pain, the doctors say. The best girls are extraordinary. The photographs ensure it. Her attacks, they say, are always imminent. We, too, are always imminent. We are always on the verge; the difference is the best girls are fluent in the language of their pain.

The photographic plates are heavy. They make a sound when the photographer changes them. *Clunk, clunk,* we are the girl standing on the platform, naked in her boots. She is no longer in the world, but where is she? The photographer underneath his tent as she waits to become a ghost. Standing there in her boots, her back to the camera, the wind of her mind blows past, then a tiredness like death rushes through her. Sometimes there are auras, luminous streaks of light on the plate. That is her, too. Years later, someone will hold in their hands a version of her she will never see. Even her secrets belonged to them. Still, after she is gone, she will be here still.

Photographic Service
Voucher for the photograph of M. Legrand

Room: Rayer

Age: 28

Birthplace: Loudun

Photograph nos: 3328, 3329, 3330, 3331

Stereoscope

Projection

Proofs: two on each side

Diagnosis

Hysteria, hemianesthesia

Information

Without being able to explain why, patient used a scissor to cut off the nipple of her left breast.

Occurred following a violent emotion.

6 September 1871

The Inclination to Believe

Is the story of Geneviève we have provided the truth?
We are very inclined to believe that it is.

>—*Iconographie photographique de la Salpêtrière,*
> vol. 1 (1877)

YOU EMERGE RELUCTANTLY on the photographic plate. Your hair parted in the middle; long, lumpy braids punctuated by thin-ribboned bows. A third bow perches on top of your head, an afterthought. Your flat mouth. Your crumpled chin. One eyebrow interrupted, as if you shaved a line through it to stop its progress. Earrings dangle from your small ears; once, someone thought it was a good idea to adorn you. In this first photograph, you don't yet know they have a name for your pain or that the stages of hysteria are called, collectively, the passionate attitudes. With great effort, you summon a body for the photographer.

You weren't the photogenic one. That was Augustine. Still, there is the fortuitous coincidence of your godliness and your hometown of Loudun, famous for its demonic possessions. In particular, Joan of the Angels, mother superior of the Ursuline Order, to whom Saint Joseph appeared after a final rough exorcism. That you walked the same earth as Joan of the Angels is useful; you hear the promise it holds in the way the doctors discuss the she who is you. Serpentine sentences laced with optimism wound into science. With your birth in Loudun, the doctors make sense of your life; with that detail, your life becomes a story with a beginning, a middle, and, somewhere up ahead, an end.

In the photograph, you look sideways out of a face a paler white than your blouse, which looks more like a billowy straitjacket, but that comes later. You may not have been the pretty one, but soon you will be known as the escape artist of the city of incurable women; it was said you could rip a straitjacket to pieces with your teeth.

You can't remember them all, the various stages of hysteria. Ecstasy, though, you know by heart. You have never not known it. The pose blurs your face, plumps your lips, ungrims the line of your mouth. Your hands clasped in prayer, you look up in the air, but you are here on the ground, filling your body like a sail. The photograph makes a body out of your godly imagination. Your inclination to ecstasy was your ticket out of the ragged stench of the room full of other women. You were chosen by the doctors, lifted up, slipped between clean sheets in a private room with a window you can open or close. Surely, they thought, everyone would want the sort of quiet space in which one's thoughts might wander.

Where did your thoughts go?

You were an orphan, left in the deposit box for babies at the Loudun Hospital on January 2, 1843; your parents too poor to care for you; or you were a scandal; or maybe everyone was dead. Of 181 children born in Loudun that year, only half survived, and one of them was you. You were the first entry of that year in the town's registry. An *enfant trouvé*, a found child, a foundling, which suggested a place you were supposed to be but weren't. You would be lost, then found, then lost again. Later—after the foster families and the nuns, after the stint hauling coal and wood in the home of Monsieur L.—your belly began to swell. You threw yourself around the room and hoarded belladonna pills, but they brought you back from death to save the child, who turned out to be imagined. Lost, then found, then lost again, you began to walk as if you could walk right out of that body so insistent on living.

Expert fugitive, you walked from Paris to Toulouse; when you returned, you were pregnant again, but this time the baby was not imagined. You called her Desirée, the desired one. You walked from Paris to Avallon to visit her after she was adopted as a foundling, though she had never been lost. How far is it, you wonder as you walk to find your daughter, the distance between lost and found? For miles, your feet step and step and step as you consider the way lost suggests you have disappeared altogether, when aren't you still somewhere, the way so often you're somewhere else not here, or here, or here?

You were detained by Prussian officers, and Desirée remained found in another town, unreachable. Who knows how many miles to who knows where, after which you returned, who knows why, with a very small dog. You walked from Paris to Loudun, to walk again the same earth Joan of the Angels walked over two hundred years ago. Most of what you know about Joan of the Angels the doctors told you—the handsome ghost spotted in her chambers; the writhing on the ground, shouting obscenities, until her sister nuns saw similar handsome ghosts, until crowds gathered to see the satanic possessions; the way she wasn't content with being possessed by Satan, and so the iron-boned, shape-shifting beast Behemoth, who arrived as a rhinoceros or maybe even a dinosaur, and Leviathan, too, rose from the sea. Chaos monsters filled her until only an exorcism so rough it nearly killed her could expel them. Once she threw off the demons, she accused a local priest of acting as Satan's accomplice. Before he was set on fire, the doctors tell you eagerly, his legs were crushed with Spanish boots, those divine instruments of torture. For years, the priest had seduced local widows and unhappy wives (except for the old and ugly ones). There are miles on the road back to Paris from Loudun when dusk light flickers its admiration through the trees at the way Joan of the Angels conjured the chaos monsters, then became one herself.

Because you were born in the same place as that conjurer of chaos, the doctors are able to make a shape of your life, one that can be seen from a distance; from deep inside this thing called your life, there is no shape. There is never enough stillness to make a shape; there is only spilling and more spilling, and pouring back and forth. When Joan of the Angels toured the country with her sacred shirt stained with Joseph's ointment, the pilgrims fell to their knees. When you touched the dirt where Joan of the Angels walked, you fell open. You spilled over and you spilled over.

You gathered a handful of that long-ago dirt trod by Joan of the Angels when you were eight, tucked it into your skirts, tucked it into a little pouch you kept with you always and, when you were grown and returned to Loudun, you gathered more long-ago dirt in the little pouch and walked it back to Paris, hid it under your bed, all of your beds, walked it from Paris to Le Quesnoy, from Le Quesnoy to Bois-d'Haine, walked it all the way to the cottage of the girl stigmatic. She, like you, suffered from what the doctors called the disease of faith. They called her the Belgian mystic; you called her your sister. Her bruises matched yours from being thrown around the room by demons; like you, she was visited by the chaos monsters, who one night cracked your skull on the foot of your bed. Like you, she had always known ecstasy by heart.

In the photograph called *Ecstasy*, you clasp your hands in prayer, palms warm with the miracle of your own blood. When you clasp your hands, you clasp the miraculous hand of Joan of the Angels, and all the hands of the pilgrims who traced the names—Jesus, Mary, Joseph—etched into her hand; you clasp the bleeding hands of the Belgian mystic, your sister. When you arrived at her cottage, they wouldn't let you inside. Why should they care you'd walked all that way? There were pilgrims who had walked farther to be in her presence. But you didn't need to go inside to do what you came to do. When it was dark, you pulled the pouch from your skirt, sprinkling that long-ago dirt trod by Joan of the Angels outside the cottage door so all of you could walk the same patch of earth.

The ghost of Louise rising up in Joan, the ghost of Louise rising up in you, risen and rising still; all your bodies, ghost-filled. Bodies, you think, are like haunted houses. You walk and you walk and you walk in your body so insistent on living. You walk as if you could walk right out of it, but bodies, we are in them.

You are a quick study. By now, you've learned in order to be a star at the Salpêtrière you must not be cured. A star performs. The illness written on your body for everyone to read; to keep your private room, you will write it and write it and write it. You will carve the names into your arm as Joan of the Angels did—Jesus, Mary, and Joseph. Or perhaps, simply, Desirée. Your daughter is gone, but aren't you the desired one now? If you need to, you will bleed and bleed. There may be a cure in curiosity, but there is no cure for it. The doctors write a chapter about you for their book, called "Succubus." A chaos monster in beautiful woman's clothing who fucks men while they sleep. You are a special succubus, possessed by an incubus; incubated by the nocturnal lover Monsieur X., with whom you describe long nights of talking and kissing and voluptuous sensations. *Her sick imagination*, the doctors write, *has created an entire novel.*

In the photograph, you cast your eyes down. Wearing a black veil, you hold what appears to be a box of light. Your mourning disguise, one more escape. You were not the photogenic one, but in your costume of grief, you are beautiful.

There you are.

Are you there?

Then you are gone.

DEATH OF A QUEER BEING.
From London Truth

Death has just put an end, at the village of
Bois d'Haine, in Belgium, to the sufferings of a
strange being, Louise Lateau, whose singular case
has puzzled many a doctor. She was called "La
Stygmatisée," the Catholics declaring that every
Friday blood flowed from wounds visible on her
hands, her feet, and her side in remembrance of
the Crucifixion. This "miracle" attracted in-
numerable sight-seers, whose contributions were
sufficient to enable the practical showman to re-
build the little village church and parsonage in
most luxurious style.

August 12, 1876

Dear Sir,

I am taking the liberty to write you on the subject of a patient who interests you very much: I am talking about the hystero-epileptic, Geneviève L. As she was traveling through Quesnoy, she was overcome by an attack of hystero-epilepsy that lasted from six in the evening until one in the morning and was only stopped with ovarian compression.

Before her attack, she had stopped in a cabaret, where she had, I am told, made some untoward remarks, and, because she had been drinking about a half liter of beer with people of even looser reputation than she, this was enough, in the eyes of the village inhabitants, for her to be taken for a drunk, for a woman who deserved not the least pity. This impression was in no way helped by a doctor who had little knowledge of nervous ailments.

When I saw her, she was in the throes of one of her attacks, with swelling of the abdomen, intermittent contractures, delirious reason, hallucinations, etc. I quickly ruled out pregnancy and epilepsy. It was by recalling your wise lessons that I was led to practice an ovarian compression. Rapidly brought back to herself, Geneviève narrated her history to me, and I was happy to have spared this girl the humiliation and the more-than-malicious criticism that had buzzed in my ears. Given the cruelty of some people's ineptitude, it is satisfying for me to recount to you this incident, to prove to you the devotion and interest that you inspire, and to take this opportunity to acknowledge my debt to you.

Geneviève remained with me for one day, and despite my insistence that she return to Paris, she said that she wanted to go and say hello "to her sister Louise Lateau" as she called her, not without reason.

Her Godly Imagination

AFTER YOU WERE DENIED ENTRY to the famous cottage, you decided you would sleep under a nearby tree. The little cottage in Bois-d'Haine where she lived with her mother and her sisters was like all the others you'd passed between Mons and Charleroi—whitewashed, green shutters, red-tiled roof. You'd walked all the way from Paris; still, how could you sleep with the whisper of her blood seeping from her holy feet into the earth, tunneling through dirt? The heat of your back drew it up to you. Lying under the tree, you watched through fall-stripped branches the clouds make the shape of her wounds—on her feet, her hands, her wrists. The most recent one on her shoulder signified Jesus' burden as He carried the cross to Mount Golgotha.

When you arrived earlier that afternoon, the curé asked for your letter from the church. *Pilgrims are required to make written requests.* You suspected every word out of his mouth—*pass the salt, it looks like rain, amen*—sounded like an explanation. He nodded his head in the direction of the other pilgrims tiptoe-peering through the window, lumping you in with the other letterless people. *My sister, my sister.* You didn't speak the words out loud, but you thought them in the direction of the cottage. You hadn't yet figured out what else to say, though you had searched for words as you walked north through cities and villages, and then you were in another country. *My sister, my sister,* the rhythm of your feet. She was renowned by then. The doctors told you the stories everyone knew. You told them to yourself as you walked. She was born into the same wrong world seven years after you. In the midst of dying all around her, she was always almost dying. Ten weeks after she was born, her father died, peeled away layer by layer by small-pox, until there were no more layers. When she and her sisters and her mother fell ill, too, the neighbors fled, afraid. Weeks later, a man who had worked with her father at the foundry discovered them; she was the half-dead baby girl wrapped in dried-out bandages. At age four, she nearly drowned in a pond. At eleven, she ministered to the sick with her sister Adelina. This was after she'd mastered the catechism, after her First Communion. She and Adelina watched over the neighbors, who, after fleeing, returned to the village and fell ill not with smallpox, as they'd feared, but with cholera, which had not even occurred to them. She and Adelina carried their neigh-bors' coffins on their backs to the cemetery. At fourteen, a cow trampled her back into crookedness. Before she was eighteen, she'd had the last rites administered to her three times. When she was finished almost dying, she began to bleed. She never bled the way other girls bled; she was a holy faucet.

My sister, my sister. Near the end of your walk from Paris, though still there were only those two words, they meant more. What other words were there? That's what you'd come here to find out. *My sister, my sister,* past the village of Manage, skirting the borders of the great Belgian coalfield, past the railway sta-tion, through orchards and gardens until the cottages became scattered and there were no regular roads. Then there you were on your back underneath a tree, watching cloud wounds, straining to hear the words in the blood whisper seeping into the dirt while *your sister, your sister,* she who ate nothing but one Communion wafer a day, peed two teaspoons in a week, never shat, never slept, stood barefoot on the beaten-earth floor, which was the very same earth against which you pressed your back, except the house built around where she stood said this is now a floor. Her sisters Rosina and Adelina were there, her mother, too. *My sister, my sister,* the only words you had you sent into the ground, willing them up through her feet where she stood bleeding in the ten-foot-square room built especially for her. She had abandoned her sewing machine hours ago.

The first Friday it happened, pain in her hands and her feet; a tingling encircled her head. The second Friday, the local priest, to whom she confessed the pain and the tingling and the drops of blood, said, Put it out of your mind. The third Friday, the blood flowed freely. Tell no one, the priest said, so she told her mother, who worried that it had something to do with the trampling cow. She loved her mother, but often she wondered what she was thinking. She looked at her mother as any eighteen-year-old girl would. Every Friday since, she bled from her palms, her feet, her sides, her forehead. She bled and bled. She had been bleeding for years. She bled until there was no one who didn't want to hear about it, even, especially, the local priest, who said tell no one. Tell everyone is what everyone did.

Only pilgrims with letters from the church are permitted, the curé repeated when you looked at him the way your sister had looked at her mother when she wondered did her bleeding have something to do with the trampling cow. Did he think you had lost your hearing as well as the letter? You suspected a fee. There was usually money involved when women bled for God. But you didn't open your mouth, fearing it was also your alleged beer breath that had him lumping you in with the letterless pilgrims. Why waste what remained of the taste of beer on your tongue, never mind your breath, on this godless man of God? You weren't drunk, you'd protested in that tavern a town or four back. They suspected every word out of your mouth—*hello, nice weather, I love you*—sounded like protest. Whether you're drunk or not isn't the point, said the man who threw you out. You wanted to know what was the point. You really, really wanted to know, you said. A woman alone, he began, but did not finish. These men explaining things to you had started to sound alike. *Pass the salt, it looks like rain, amen.* All those miles, you had dropped the point on the side of the road, somewhere in the dust, when you squatted behind a tree to pee. Maybe the point was the dust. You didn't tell him any of this. He had shut the door at the end of his unfinished sentence. Even if he hadn't shut the door, you wouldn't have told him, the way you wouldn't have told him about the pouch of dirt you brought from centuries ago, dirt touched by the feet of Joan of the Angels, feet blistered from the fire that burned her from the inside out. The doctors—*Pass that salt. Look at that rain. Amen*—so determined to find a point so dry all you had to do was look at it and it went up in smoke. In search of that point, theologians and scientists put ammonia up your sister's nose, shouted in her ear, ran needles through her arm, shocked her with volts of electricity. The vicar general of the diocese wrapped her gloved hands in linen bags tied with rope to show it was not a trick. It was not a trick. *My sister, my sister.* She just bled and bled.

Through the fall-stripped branches, rings of clouds made the blood-beaded coronet that appeared every Friday on her forehead. The beads that fell and bloomed on the fabric underneath the sewing machine over which she bent her head, as she had been instructed to do by the observing theologians. *Continue work on the days of the week that aren't Friday, and on Friday, too. Ward off ecstasy with the power rendered powerless by ecstasy, proof of the irresistible lure of ecstasy.* You didn't need proof. *No salt no rain amen.* You, too, lived in a body that filled weekly with holy yearning and a desire that unbound you from the world where the theologians and scientists lived. It unfurled you tender into a place where there were no words except those you made with your body, irresistible as the place itself. You knew what it was to tumble back again from the risen other world into this one, to land stiffly, arms locked at your sides, icy hands, face pale and cold with sweat, your pulse thrillingly undetectable. The death rattle in your throat never lasted the fifteen minutes the doctors who loved to count the minutes reported hers had; still, she was your sister.

And so, when he turned you away, you said nothing to the curé. You would not waste your beer breath protesting in the name of devotion or love. *Hello, nice weather, I love you.* There was a time you wanted to be as complete as the photographs the doctors took of you, but from within the endless spilling that was your life, you had come to understand that aspiring to be still as a photograph was to fail and fail; still, you were beginning to suspect that aspiring was all there was, so why stop? The distance from inside your spilling to the spilling inside other people was the distance you'd walked from Paris to the cottage, multiplied by your lifetime and theirs.

You'd walked at least that many miles trying to explain to the doctors the visits you'd received from that certain Monsieur X. (the name the doctors gave him), who visited you in the middle of the night to conduct medical experiments, which caused, as he explained (*Amen, it's raining salt*), genital sensations. You required no explanation. You just said thank you. (*Hello! Nice weather! I love you!*) Sometimes you and he had violent quarrels. Sometimes you got along well. According to the doctors, Monsieur X. was imaginary. What you knew was there was more pleasure with him in the middle of the night than you'd ever had with any man. The doctors said they admired your imagination. If it was your imagination whose fingers stroked you slick until you came then you admired your imagination, too. When they continued to ask what was the point of this imagined lover, you just smiled.

No sharp edges, blood rolls around and over all the points. *My sister, my sister.* She went to church every day except Friday; on that day, the Blessed Sacrament was brought to her on a platter held aloft by the local priest, who had said tell no one.

When the curé told you to leave if you couldn't produce a letter from the Church, you didn't tell the curé that you wouldn't be able to distinguish true holy oils from fake ones, either, if they were waved in front of your face, nor would you be able to detect the fragment of consecrated host in a priest's pocket or the snuck-in sacred vessel or the sacred relic—the finger of a beloved saint wrapped in a bow, for example— tucked away in a satchel. Joy trembled your body, too, but why put a ribbon-wrapped sacred finger in a satchel? Why wrap a ribbon around a bone in the first place? Though it did give you good ideas for your funeral. You wouldn't bother to ask, the same way you wouldn't explain how when joy trembled you nearly to death, there was no asking or explaining, no pitiful effort at words. *My sister, my sister.* No words for the no feel-ing at all of their needle passed through her arm. *Do you feel this?* Or the sensationless sensation of their hot wax not burn-ing her flesh. *Do you feel it burning your flesh?* Declarations with question marks placed at the end for the sake of the audience. The doctors knew what you would say (*I feel nothing*), the way the theologians knew what your sister would tell them after she returned from ecstasy (*I remember nothing*). Declarations with questions marks at the end of them for the sake of those pilgrims who had letters telling them this was God's work. The body upon whom God was working? That body was for no one's sake and forsaken.

At the end of your walk from Paris, when you arrived at the cottage like the other cottages but this one with your sister and her whispering blood inside, it came to you. You would stand before her. You would announce, *We are the same.* You would hand her the pouch filled with centuries-old dirt trod by Joan of the Angels's ancient feet. Joan of the Angels was the same as both of you. All of you, born into the wrong world. You longed to bring her this news, but you heard in her blood's whisper the way she already knew. No explanation, no protest. No pitiful effort at words required.

As afternoon turned into evening, the curé grew exasperated with the letterless tiptoeing peerers, their faces fogging the window of the cottage. This is a house of God, not a cabaret, he shouted. By then, you'd already done him the favor of banishing yourself to lie underneath the tree. You were exhausted by the endless division of the world into the high and the low, the this but not that, the that but not this. The house of God or the cabaret, as if God lived only in one place and never went out for a drink and some company. What kind of life was that? When ecstasy overtook you, when it trembled you the way Monsieur X. trembled you so well, you knew God filled you the same way He filled the men who offered you the last of their beer the way He filled the man who kicked you out of the tavern the way

He filled the curé insisting on a letter to grant you an audience with your sister so full of God she bled all Friday long.

The cloud wounds have seeped into the sky, absorbed into darkness like her blood into the earth. You read an article once in which she was described as an untutored peasant girl. *Imagination she has none*, it said. After the curé shooed away the pilgrims who lacked letters, after he went home, you slipped through the dark to the lip of the famous cottage you were never permitted to enter. You opened the pouch and, ashes to ashes, scattered the dirt trod by Joan of the Angels on the threshold.

How could you have slept underneath those fall-stripped branches? *Your sister, your sister*, the whisper of her blood was not made of the pitiful effort of words. It whispered the grit and silk of pond water between her toes, the soft fabric held in place with the tips of her fingers and the prick of the sewing machine when her attention drifted, the smell of Adelina's neck where she burrowed as she went to sleep, though always she woke up on the other side of the bed, legs entangled in Rosina's, chewing her fingernails even as she slept. It whispered her hair waving like the plants on the muddy bottom of a river and the musky warmth of the cow's slow heaving side, where she and her sisters buried their faces when it lay on the ground. It whispered the sky swallowing itself in darkness and the cloud wounds turning into stars. All through the night, it whispered love and countless other things for which there is no translation.

determines a contracture of the right arm half flexed across the back; —left arm half flexed across the front; —legs in extension; —clubfooted. An attack provoked by compressing hysterogenic zones will stop the contracture.

The best position for a successful demonstration is for the patient to be stretched out horizontally on the floor, or, if possible, on a mattress. . . .Then the doctor, with one knee on the ground, plunges his closed fist into [her ovarian region]. Most important, he must call on all of his forces in order to vanquish the rigidity of the abdominal muscles. 24 Nov.

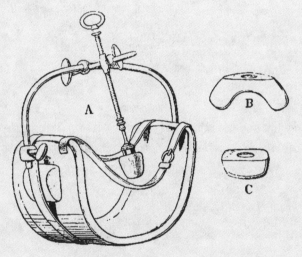

—During his lesson, M. Charcot provoked an artificial contracture of the tongue and larynx (particularly excitable musculature during hypnosis). We were able to stop the contracture of the tongue using the compression belt, but not that of the larynx, which rendered the patient voiceless. From the 25th to the 30th of November, we applied a powerful magnet, which

Photographic Service
Voucher for the photograph of M. Wittmann

Room: Cruvellier

Age: 18

Residence: 2, rue du Cherche-Midi

Photograph nos: 1245, 1246, 1247, 1248

Stereoscope

Projection

Proofs: two on each side

Diagnosis

Hysteria, paralysis of the face, eyes, feet

Information

Tall (five feet, three inches) and corpulent (154 pounds). Blond, lymphatic complexion. White and freckled skin, large breasts. Scar on the upper outside part of her left thigh.

6 May 1877

In all investigation we have to learn the lesson of patience. I am among the first to recognize that Shakespeare's words hold good today—"There are more things in heaven and earth, Horatio, than are dreamt of in thy philosophy."

—Jean-Martin Charcot
"The Faith That Cures" (1892)

Father, Ether, Sea

Like all of the hysterics from the belle époque, she seemed
to deny her past, and when questioned about the slight-
est detail from that part of her life, she responded with a
refusal tinged with anger.

—A. Baudouin
"Quelques souvenirs de la Salpêtrière" (1925)

WHEN THE HUNGER COMES, bread, onions, artichokes,
herring—I douse it all with vinegar and stuff my face
until I cannot breathe.

I was born to go nowhere, the doctors said. Still, every
day, there is a choice and I make it. I go somewhere. What
next?

Let me begin again.

When I lost my hand, all I wanted was the ether. With
amyl nitrite, a burst of kaleidoscopic colors too quickly
gone; with chloroform, dreams both pleasant and painful
but mostly painful. With ether, agreeable and voluptuous
dreams, a brightening, the infinite moving through me. I feel
nothing, which isn't nowhere at all. In the days when I was
queen, I'd sip from stolen bottles—the doctors often careless,
leaving the bottle after they'd applied the cloth. Twelve years
after the great doctor's death, the death of the diagnosis, the
death of my queendom, and so on and whatnot, no one cares

to put me under. Now I work in the radiology lab. I work in it and it has worked in me. Still, for everything sharpened, everything crisped, I look everywhere for the little bottles. When I find them, in that expanding light, something floats up from my past, that great well of surprise. The apple stolen from a basket of fruit and candy a visitor brought to a patient at the Hôpital Temporaire, where I worked years or decades ago as a ward girl. Only slightly bruised, that apple is still the sweetest I've ever tasted.

Today, the new doctor wandering the radiology lab startled me with a question and my father floated up out of that well. There he was, promising, as he forever was, to take us to the sea, by which he meant the Seine, that dirty river. Even the blocks of ice bobbing in it that winter were dirty. It doesn't count, my brothers and I would say. What exactly were we counting? We'd never seen anything else.

They say those attacks were simulated, the new doctor whispered to the intern I had recently spurned, as if it were all a secret. The new doctor has a droopy, yearning mustache. A young man but terrible posture, all of him a little wilted. He nodded his head in my direction, curious as the rest. Tucked inside his sentence, questions: *Did you and the great doctor or didn't you? Why did you tear the linens? Why did you break the plates?* And questions he didn't have the imagination to ask: *Do you dream about your missing arm? What is the difference between abandoned and unfortunate? Why did your father throw you out the window?*

Bread, onion, artichoke, herring, vinegar, vinegar, vinegar, vinegar.

Let me begin again.

Was it soon after he lost his job as a carpenter that my

father piled my brothers and me on a train to the sea? He'd found piecemeal work with a milliner who wanted him to go to Dunkirk to visit a business on his behalf in Saint-Omer, where he hoped to sell some of his hats on consignment. Maybe my father knew an engineer who sneaked us into a compartment? That day felt—it feels—like the beginning of everything, not the end. Surely my mother could not have given up a day of work, particularly since my father had been for a while between jobs. I wish I could come, she said, but why would she wish that? She was glad to be rid of us for a few days. Maybe, even fleetingly, she wished us gone for good, because when we wish these things, how can we ever know it might actually come true?

We lived next to one of the largest metalworking factories in Paris. Outside were piles of thick iron sheets, waiting always to be moved. In the winter, my brothers and I watched as men chipped ice from them. Next door to the factory was the ironworks with its puddling furnace, where my brothers would eventually work, loading pig iron into a wheelbarrow, heaving it into the furnace, removing the slag. One day, not long after he took us to the sea, my father wandered in. Someone pulled the chain that opened the scorching furnace door, and he tried to crawl inside. The men working the furnace pulled him back. Only his pants caught fire, which disappointed him greatly. The delirium lasted weeks. It landed him in bed number 40 of the Saint Charles Ward, where a nun gave my mother a vial containing six drops of some mysterious thing. After that, he was carted off to an asylum, never to be heard from again.

They say you were only making fools of them, the droopy, yearning doctor said again, as if my lost hand meant

I was deaf, too. He sidled up gently, not understanding it was never gentleness that brought me around in the amphitheater. Bright lights, strips of magnesium, whistles. There was an enormous gong. Bang that, I'm yours.

The doctors? he added, as if my silence meant confusion.

He wanted the truth, as if it were a bottle of camphor or a bone. I kept my eyes on my work. I said nothing and he said nothing more, perched on the edge of his imagination, where I was on my knees. Who among us hasn't been? His eyes threw heat, not altogether unpleasant.

One of those hysterics who has had her moment of fame, said the spurned intern, who was never not watching. After I wouldn't let him maneuver me into the closet a second time, he would have liked to perform the amputation himself. Women have their fragility, but men are so easily wounded. He had rough, unspecific hands. I had only the burns then. That was when I first began working in the radiology lab. I hadn't yet lost a single finger.

This is not the amphitheater, I said, gesturing with my stump. It usually scared him off. There was a time I would have said, Oh, leave me alone; every night I am put under I no longer know what I'm doing or what I've become, but that was a long time ago, when I would lie down in the courtyard for hours and refuse to get up.

She's better since she lost the hand, the intern said, not as though he wanted me to hear, as though I wasn't there at all.

I'm missing a hand, I said. I'm not deaf.

Dead, not deaf, the intern said. Subtle he is not. Still, there are days when I would rather be as lost as my hand and the era when I was queen. All of it vanished—where did it go?

That's when the droopy, yearning doctor startled me. What comforts you? he asked. His curiosity was a door opening. The intern took him by the arm, steered him elsewhere in the lab. What are you on about? the intern asked him. Don't get mixed up in that. His own curiosity so often swerved into meanness. Still, the new doctor's question lingered. It lingers. I misinterpreted his mustache. Yearning? Maybe, but not drooping, not wilted.

Let me begin again.

From Paris to Dunkirk, did my father tell us stories as the train heaved in and out of stations on its way to the sea? After he climbed into the furnace, my brothers said everything he told us wasn't true, but what is life if not the lies we tell about it? Truth is not camphor or a bone. The stories we tell, adjacent at best. Even the moon is a liar; it appears to be waxing when it is waning, waning when it is waxing. When I was a plastic mass of flesh and bones molded at the will of the doctors—the queen!—onto which the most fantastic emotions could be imprinted, truth seemed beside the point. They said we had an essentially perverse nature. That our impulse was to steal, falsely accuse, set things on fire. We had a need to lie for no reason and to no end. They said this as if it were some great discovery, as if it had nothing to do with them. They had never lied out of desperation, or just because they could? They hypnotized us and told us ammonia was rose water, charcoal was chocolate, a top hat was a baby to be cradled. Who among us hasn't tried to wring a little fun out of the struggle?

Let me begin again.

The hospital has always been a museum full of dead things. When the great doctor died, he became one of the dead things. Still, there he is, hanging on the wall in the painting by André Brouillet, nine by thirteen feet, *the greatest success of the Salon of 1887*, according to a review in *The Temp*. A million sets of eyes came to the Palais de l'Industrie to see *A Clinical Lesson at the Salpêtrière*. Twenty-seven men (doctors, philosophers, two novelists, an art critic who was also a collector, the artist himself) and two nurses, larger than life-size, gather around a swooning woman with spectacular bosoms, a woman who is me. By the time the painting was finished, I'd been there ten years; the Marie I was when I arrived painted over, and there was Blanche, all swoon and fiery revelation. My face says *tragedy, mystery*; my clenched fist, the contracture—that long-gone hand alive as the long-gone great doctor—says *hysteria*. How odd to see the shape someone makes of you when a whole life of days can go by, a hunger with no shape at all. The gap between how we are measured and how we feel—isn't that life?

The painting, born from a desire to look; in it, I look. The eyes on the back of my head look onto one of those endless Parisian rains that double-blur the days. The slick courtyard stones, damp and cold as the stone floor of the church where my mother sent me for confession as a girl. What next? the priest asked. What next, my child? Inattention to prayers, the sin of gluttony, no end to what next. *What next?* In the painting, the doctor cradling my swoon, does he feel my child's heart racing ahead of itself, racing up ahead years later to what next? I was an imaginative child, but never could I have imagined my way into that painted swoon. My searching child's heart, like my father's when he was a boy, raced ahead, curious about its future. One day, not able to read a sign on the door, he walked into a random home to beg a scrap of bread. The home turned out to be the office of the mayor, who walked him directly to the jail for violating the local ordinance against begging. There wasn't one against not being able to read.

What next? What next? Ticking inside me, a hunger clock. Bread, onions, artichokes, herring, vinegar, vinegar, vinegar, vinegar.

Let me begin again.

My father, I loved him more than anyone else in the world, my father told us, as if we were not his children, but strangers he'd met on that train. His father was a miller. His mother died when he was a baby. That he was ever a baby, that seemed strange enough; that he grew from a baby into a boy, stranger still. We listened, his life rushing by us like the world outside the train windows. One day, he was that boy and he was leaving school. He saw people running toward the mill where his father worked. There must be something extraordinary! What could it be? He was thrilled by the possibilities, that wide-open feeling of anything, anything, before you understand that anything, anything contains everything from delight to wreckage. He would find his father. His father would tell him what it was. Up ahead, his uncle fell to the ground. When he saw how badly the mill had been damaged, he fainted rather than see more. The windmill was not turning. A lightning bolt had struck one of the vanes and it broke apart, trapping my father's father underneath. People led my father away and he never saw his father again. You are abandoned, his aunt said; you must come live with us now. What are you saying? his uncle shouted. He isn't abandoned, he insisted, only unfortunate.

This distinction, my father said to me and my brothers, it is everything. I am not abandoned, only unfortunate.

You are not abandoned, only unfortunate, he said when he gathered me up after he threw me out the window. Whenever he said it, he was telling our future, mine and my brothers'. He was telling us how to live after he was gone, which would be sooner than any of us thought.

Let me begin again.

What next? My curious heart races ahead.

The placid and delectable Alsatian, that's what they called me when I arrived at the hospital twenty-eight years ago. Placid? I could put it on. Delectable? Perhaps. But Alsatian? I was born in Paris, but it did not fit their story made not of camphor, not of bone, these doctors, these emperors of anecdote. The queen of gongs and tremors and tuning forks began in the City of Lights. When the lights sharpen to the point of sound, take me to the city of shadows. Bread, onions, herring, artichoke, vinegar, vinegar, vinegar, vinegar.

The first thing they wrote when I arrived was *tall, corpulent, blond, lymphatic complexion, white and freckled skin, very large breasts, scar on the upper outside of left thigh.*

The first thing I did when I arrived was leave. Eighteen years old, I sneaked out of the hospital. I was gone for hours, but I never left the Grands Boulevards. Where would I have gone? Those first nights in the hospital, I was not yet Blanche, only Marie. I cried out in my sleep, Blanche! Blanche! Come quick! This is what they told me. This was before the ether; still, I have no memory of those nights. Was Blanche a dead sister? they wondered. I thought, Well, somewhere there's a dead sister named Blanche, but she's not mine. I have two brothers, who might be dead, but I did not tell them that. I

love the name Blanche. It's always made me think, Bosoms.
Even now I have spectacular bosoms. I became Blanche and
then I became the queen. Throughout Europe, the doctor
became great, but I was the queen, and even he, in all his
greatness, understood the queen was greater.

From here to there, the great doctor traced my story,
a story he made out of things I remembered, or dreamed,
or things I dreamed I remembered. He traced the line from
there to here. Camphor! Bone! The seizures and convulsions
that left me partially deaf and mute as a child. Apprenticed
to a furrier at the age of twelve. In that house, I dropped
everything I tried to hold. The furrier's wife, believing I was
doing it on purpose, made me pay for the things I broke.
By the end, I was in *their* debt. Two years later, the furrier
attacked me. I ran all the way home to my mother, who
allowed me to work with her—she was a laundress—by the
Seine. The mariners and dockers mistook us for prostitutes,
despite the heavy loads of wet clothing we carried. Every day,
they followed us home, until the day my mother couldn't get
out of bed. Of the first weeks after she died, the only thing I
remember are dark rooms. Soon after, my two brothers were
placed in foster homes and I went back to the furrier. I'd lost
my virginity by then to a boy I liked who worked for a jew-
eler. He had deliberate hands, specific fingers. Eight months
after I started working again for the furrier, I woke up with
the shakes and broke every plate in the house. When I ran
away, a nun from the convent on the rue du Cherche-Midi
took me in. I think I would have made a good nun, but then I
would never have become bosomy Blanche. I'd still be dusty
old Marie. Two months later, I had a fit in the laundry room
and tore all the linens. It was then I came to the Salpêtrière,

hired first as a ward girl, a few days later admitted to the noninsane epileptic ward.

The doctors assumed my father was one of the men down by the Seine who followed my mother home. The curiosity of those men, like that of the intern, often swerved into cruelty. I kept some things to myself. I keep some things from myself.

Let me begin again.

There are endless photographs of us in this museum of dead things. Before I worked in the radiology lab, I worked briefly as an assistant in the photography lab. *Catalepsy: Provoked Pose*, the photograph is called. There it is again, my lost hand, not lost at all. There were days I needed the bright light, the incandescent strip, the whistle, the gong; then there were days it came unbidden. I came unbidden. In the photograph, my left arm is raised. There it is again, my long-gone hand not gone at all (camphor! bone!) but double-blurred, like Paris rain out a painted window. The great doctor said I was a kind of statue, and it is true, I could be when the doctors were especially forgetful. A half bottle, I could hold a position for hours. They raised my arms above my head like a ballerina's, but the way my head is turned, gazing up at my hand, that was my decision. The curve of my hand reminded me of a wax doll the woman who ran the laundry where my mother worked once gave me. A ballerina with beautiful hands, tiny and perfect. A fine vein like the stripped branch of a tree in winter reaches up the inside of my wrist. How to describe the feeling of being only body? That ether feeling of nothingness that wasn't nothing. I always had beautiful hands. My fingers, long and lovely. The cup of my own palm holds my gaze; it holds me there, in its world. The amphitheater, the hospital, the city, the country—there is infinite, glorious space. My mother, my father, my brothers are there, still. There it is, the world, not lost at all. Though maybe it's true what they said about me. What they say still. I am in pieces.

When the train arrived at the port on the North Sea in Dunkirk, did we go to the shipyards? Did my brothers and my father strike up a conversation with some of the men working the docks? Did they talk the way certain men talk about things they are encountering for the first time, conjuring solid facts? The size and shape and seaworthiness of those ships—the words they found to tether the things they saw would have fascinated me. I stuck around awhile, thinking I might learn something, but then the jetty called to me. I walked out onto it. There, way out on the horizon, a boat. For hours, the boat moved across that water, so slowly it seemed not to move at all. The sea surrounding it, a glittering vision of the infinite.

Marie de Saint-Euphrasie Pelletier was born surrounded by the sea, on the island of Noirmoutier, in 1796, during the French Revolution, a saint who lacked the patina of age. How could she be a saint? But that was not the sort of question my mother tolerated.

Why Marie? I asked instead, when I was old enough for it to occur to me.

My mother pulled out the *Lives of the Saints*, never far from hand. Because, she read, she was *the child of the sounding sea, daughter of the suffering faith of her beloved France.*

What does it mean to be a child of the sounding sea?

You'll find out, she said.

What does the sounding sea sound like?

Maybe I gave you the wrong name.

She was a busy woman. She had no time for nonsense. Not unlike Sainte Marie, who was the foundress of the great congregation of Our Lady of Charity of the Good Shepherd of Angels and the foundress of the refuge for penitent women at Angers; who entered the Order of Our Lady of Charity of the Refuge at Tours; who was the mother superior of the house of the new congregation; who, during her thirty years as superior general, sent her sisters out to found 110 houses. *In every land beneath the sun; sisters inflamed with her own zeal.*

It's a beautiful name is all you need to know, she said over her shoulder as I trailed her through the streets, helping her to carry the heavy, wet clothing.

When I broke every plate in the furrier's house, the sound glittered like the sea. Plates and plates and plates, the glittering crashed through me. The light on the sounding sea shimmered in me where I stood on the jetty, tidal. The tides had something to do with that lying moon, my father or my brothers or one of the men by the docks said. I felt myself a part of the moon, a part of the waves. This body wasn't a problem.

What comforts you? the new doctor asked.

What did he really want to know?

Sometimes the doctors would put me to sleep and subject me to certain influences. I forgot who I was, my age, my sex, my nationality. I forgot when I was and why. I lost the idea of my late existence. Even still, I was not abandoned, only unfortunate. I was not abandoned, only unfortunate. That boat was in no hurry to get anywhere at all. Where was it going? It moves still, across the infinite, and everyone still and always here.

I appear to be waxing when I am waning, waning when I am waxing. My father never took us to the sea, only the Seine, that dirty river. Who cares?

I want to ask my father, who left this earth long ago, why is unfortunate better than abandoned? Sometimes, I stuff my mouth with vinegar-doused bread, onions, artichokes, herring, and try to forget the question; sometimes, I find the bottles, turn my insides to silk, and the question no longer matters. What question?

It's funny the details that make up a life. Born to go nowhere? No one can see the shape of a life until it's over. The great doctor traced a story with the stories I gave him, from here to there, but then he died and my life was not over yet, no *there* yet. I won't be here for *there*. I'll never know if it was nowhere I was born to go. There is only beginning and beginning. And, so.

Let me, oh let me, begin again.

There's the story of your life and then there are the parts no one can ever know. Not even you.

CASE NOTES (1878)

We used the point of a stylus to trace the name of the patient on her chest, and on her abdomen, we traced the word "Salpêtrière." This produced a red stripe that was several centimeters high, and on this band the letters appeared in relief, about two millimeters wide. Little by little the redness disappeared, but the letters persisted.

We write the name of the patient with the point of a pin across the upper part of her chest, the word "August" on each leg, and "Salpêtrière" on her abdomen. A quite large reddened stripe develops promptly; then, the letters appear in relief.

W. hid in the gardens until 11:00 at night.

PLANCHE IX.

Fig. 1.

Fig. 2.

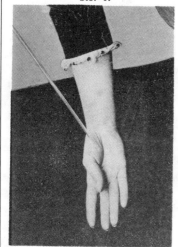

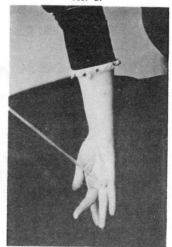

Fig. 3.

Fig. 4.

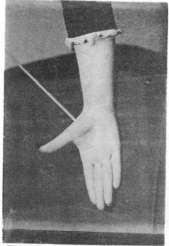

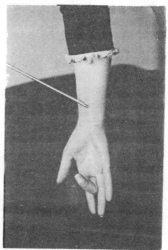

Case Notes (1885):

measles, then fever of the mucous membrane. In her convalescence, a number of abscesses.

At fourteen years, L. was tall, strong, looked as though she was seventeen or eighteen. She was placed in an English family to teach the children French. After six months living with them in England, in relative calm, she left because, she said, the London climate was harmful and she had "too much to do." At the recommendation of her mistress, she entered into another situation with another family, where she stayed eighteen months. There she was charged with the care of three children—Henry, Frank, and Christine. She lived with them sometimes in the country in the château of their grandparents, who were in their seventies. Once, while living in the château, she was left with the monsieur and the children alone. The monsieur gave her a drink, of which she did not know the name, or she did not wish to tell us. Profiting from her sleep, the monsieur abused her. On different occasions, his attempts were more and less violent; one time there was a scuffle because she saw him put powder of some kind in her food. It is difficult to get at the precise details, as she "swore to keep it a secret." During her time in England, she had jaundice for three months. What caused this, we do not know.

Menstruation began when she was sixteen years old. She reports violent pain in her loins and in her lower abdomen, which required a visit to the doctor. Menstruation began when she was sixteen but did not return again for eight to ten months. From age sixteen to age seventeen and a half, L. reports seven or eight attacks, each lasting about an hour. At the age of seventeen and a half, L. returned to Paris to live with her mother. For some time after, she said, she felt

Photographic Service
Voucher for the photograph of M. Beaudon

Room: Passage Lepic
Age: 14
Residence: unknown

Photograph nos: 2090, 2091, 2092, 2093
Stereoscope
Projection
Proofs: two on each side

Diagnosis
Saint Vitus's dance

28 December 1882

Avril Jane

Never the Same Way Twice

But then, suddenly, she departs from her own rhythm, breaks it, and creates a new one; she seems never tired, always re-inventing herself.

—PAUL-JEAN TOULET
On seeing Jane Avril dance at the
Jardin de Paris (1926)

MY UNDERSKIRTS WERE NEVER the classic white of the Moulin Rouge; the layers underneath my scarlet gown shaded deep red to shell pink. When I danced, I could take the hat off a man without using my hands. I made that bet a thousand times and never lost. The men closed their eyes and inhaled deeply, smelling their way through silk and chiffon.

Everywhere, and always, so many layers. Between the entrance and the grand ballroom, a small stage where they ran the cabaret show; next to the stage a small garden; inside the small garden, an enormous hollow elephant; inside the elephant, there were rumored to be side shows. I never went. I've always preferred gossip to the real thing. Anyway, I had the better secret. It wandered my body, refusing to tell itself even to me.

Even when I was a little girl, a walk down the street was never just a walk down the street. There was always a little extra, wanting to be shaken out. My hands conspired; my head nodded a two-beat, three-beat, four-beat rhythm; my feet stumbled over things other people could not see. What was it that wandered my body? In my bones, my muscles, through my blood, it moved. When my mother was in the mood to keep me, when I wasn't with my grandparents or the nuns, still she sent me to the post office, the grocery store, or just *get out out out*. I'd ride her temper out the door, and my own nerve storms blew me down the street. To everyone who stopped to stare, my stumbling shivering shaking sounded like *help help help*, but did they ever? People love to almost know something—whether it's what's wrong with you or what's right. They love to teeter, on the edge, on the verge, like sex, like standing in an enormous hollow elephant inside a secret garden while next door cancan girls take the hats off men's heads with only their feet.

St. Vitus's dance was the doctor's explanation for the extra shaking itself *out out out*. Even my disease wanted to dance! Saint Vitus, the saint who protected against animal attacks, oversleeping, and lightning attacks, was the patron saint of dancers, actors, and epileptics. He never protected *me* from the lightning. I was his lightning-struck dancer. It would be years before the secret moving through me found a way to express itself that didn't evoke only pity.

Get out out out. Off to the Cours Désir my mother sent me, paid for with money borrowed from the Italian marquis she claimed was my father. Every day, I got up on the high-horse bus in my bottle green dress and gray cloth boots, to the school for well-mannered girls who did not stumble, shiver, or shake. Not a one of them lightning-struck. At the Cours Désir, pastel drawing, crocheting, knitting, the gentle art of sewing the wide-open legs of desire shut. How to serve tea, should I ever serve it, how to address the president of the Republic, should I ever meet him, how to address the parish priest, should I ever go to church. Désir was the name of an old French family who had taken it upon themselves to create a convent school where young women might learn the posture and demeanor of the nuns. Nuns who, though they themselves never entertained company, were believed by this old French family to possess the necessary qualities. These same nuns said of my mother, though she never left marks on my face, *She is a woman of bad life.* No washing it away, the smell of a mother who believes she should love you but does not.

It was I who did the curtsying when she took me around to convince the Italian marquis to give her money. How to curtsy, should you ever meet the Italian marquis your mother claims is your father: right leg behind left, bent just slightly, hope for the best. In room after room of locked glass cabinets full of rare books and small Flemish paintings, carved jade figures, silk fans, I curtsied in the general direction of the man with whom my mother had, she said, conducted a relationship long enough to get her pregnant. How long was that? Even then, I understood this could mean a lot of things, including not long at all, including never. The marquis had fallen on hard times. Whenever we visited, something else had disappeared from the cabinets—a book, a fan. One by one, the paintings began to vanish, until, one day, the cabinets were bare. I sank gently one last time, right leg behind slightly bent left leg, the stumble-shiver-shake a shadow choreography. That apartment full of nothing smelled of chicory, rum, and anise, sweet herbs and flowers and smoking ham. The smell of the end, turns out, is whatever drifts over from other people's kitchens. The change in my mother's face, subtle as my curtsy—I understood that she understood there would be no point in returning, and that was the end of the Cours Désir.

During one of the times my mother decided she didn't want me, and before another of the times she decided she wanted me back, I lived with my grandparents near the Zoological Gardens. Paris had fallen to the Prussians, and German soldiers billeted at my grandparents' house. Out the window, people carted zoo animals away for food in the same carts once used to feed them; inside, I studied my grandmother's dance as she clicked around the red-tiled kitchen, negotiating the copper pans and the officers who stood by the fireplace next to the earthenware jug full of milk from a nearby farm. The officers promised to keep the jug filled as long as my grandmother, one-two-three, kept the beds made up, one-two-three, dinner on the table, one-two-three, whatever it is you need, whatever it is you need, whatever it is you need.

It was my grandmother who told me my mother gave birth to a child before me who didn't live for even one day. Was he still my brother? Was his father my father and was my father even my father if he didn't claim me? My grandmother kept on with her story, meaning no more questions. Everyone tiptoe-whispered after the child died, afraid of disturbing his eternal sleep. My grandmother made curtains out of sheets for the pauper's bed on the crowded maternity ward where my mother still lay. She lit a candle, and someone else brought a branch of boxwood, soaked it in water, declared it holy. The knell was sounded and the ward nurses gathered around the bed to pray and sprinkle the water made holy by the now-holy boxwood-branch on my dead brother. The dance of death: He hadn't lasted a day, but his life would mean something. My grandmother didn't have to say, This is part of your mother's sadness. She didn't have to say, Sadness lasts this long. Of course it does. Where would it go? It divides and divides, pieces of it taking up residence in the space behind your ear, the vein on your forehead, the crook of your neck. There it is, flickering at the corner of your eye as you shout *get out out out*. Here it is, flickering in mine.

My grandmother died, and my mother didn't want to keep me, and I stumble-shiver-shook my way into the hospital, filled with the stars of hysteria. It was a kind of Eden for me, so much in this world being relative. The buildings, the gardens, the large portals that divided the courtyards evoked a great century, giving off a majesty in the style of Louis XVI. I'd never seen dance like these women did, their bodies bending but not breaking: arched backs, clenched fists and feet, thrusting hips, winking eyes, the supple suddenly stiff, the stiff suddenly stiffer. The other women had nothing to hide from me—I was of so little consequence. By then, I knew all kinds of dances, but the dance of hysteria, it was a revelation. Like St. Vitus's dance, it was for no one, not really. The stars performed, but everybody, every *body*, has its own secrets. Seeing theirs dance made me love my own.

Some nights, the nurses read to us from *Lives of the Saints*. When you sing, you pray twice; when you read aloud, the words become a kind of dance. November 1, All Saints' Day, one of the nurses read: *In addition to those whom the Church honors by special designation, or has inscribed in her calendar, how many martyrs are there whose names are not recorded!* Oh, just you wait, I thought. *It is a holy and wholesome thought to pray for the dead, that they may be loosed from sin.* Recently departed souls, the nurses told us, are stained with sin and remain on earth to suffer punishment for their offenses. This clearly meant us. We were alive and we were dead. We would be relieved, the nurse told us, only by the intercession of the heavenly saints.

I've often thought the people who wrote the Bible were writing to remind themselves: Don't forget, here is what needs doing. This? Yes, and this, too. Aspirational, like most words strung together to make a sentence. Flip the sentences over, desire etched into its underbelly: May these words in this order be related, proximate, adjacent—as close as possible to the mind's swirling. A chasm between the thing and the expression; in that chasm, the dance. The secret moving through my body, searching for the wrong I did to make me shiver and stumble and shake. This? Was it this? This this this?

One night, there was a masked ball in the hospital's pavilion. Yellow satin Pompadour skirt, a tight-waisted bodice frilled with Valenciennes lace, my hair pinned up beneath a straw hat with flowers and a ribbon. From her own wardrobe, the great doctor's daughter disguised me as descente de la Courtille, that lady of the court returning on a carnival night in the famous pleasure gardens of Belleville. For me, more memory than make-believe. I had once been the pleasure in the pleasure gardens.

At the ball, future notables of the medical professions were in attendance. Even the great doctor himself was there. I danced with masked musketeers and princes wearing plumes and men dressed as monks. I polkaed with a knight in armor. But when the time came, something rose up in me, and I danced alone.

The secret pulsed through, seeking, finding only what was right. It teetered me on the glorious verge, singing *yes yes yes*. I was a whirlpool tunneling through the surface of a river, this stumbling shivering shaking body elegant and harmonious. What other world was there? In my reverie, I was only and ever yes.

A few days later, my mother, hearing the news of my success, rushed to retrieve me. *Get out out out,* but my body was the one place she could never throw me out of. That night, I was my own. That night, I understood my calling. Dancing solo, I created a sensation. I knew then I would love and be loved in return, and never the same way twice.

Photographic Service
Voucher for the photograph of M. Legrand

Room: Rayer
Age: 35
Birthplace: Loudun

Photograph nos: 3501, 3502, 3503, 3504
Stereoscope
Projection
Proofs: two on each side

Diagnosis
Hysteria, atrophy of the tongue (succubus)

Information
Genital sensations, nocturnal lover/demon.

6 September 1878

Case Notes (1879)

D . . . J . . . , age nineteen, a domestic, entered the Salpêtrière (service of M. Charcot) on December 2, 1879.

Her employers, with whom the patient was placed nine months ago, give us the following information: Her father, who works on farms, is a drunkard. He drinks the next day what he won the day before. Her mother died in childbirth. D. has four siblings, two sisters and two brothers. One brother, one sister, dead. The living sister, age twenty-eight, has four children; she does not have a nervous illness.

D. is small, thin (forty-eight kilograms). Her skin is very white; her mucous membranes are not very colorful. Her hair is black and abundant; she adorns herself with ribbons and spends time on her toilette. The features are regular; the physiognomy is agreeable enough, but with a certain cunning expression. She is intelligent, suspicious, whimsical. Some days, she cries or laughs without reason, chatting one day, taciturn the next. She does not want us to know anything about her intimate life, though she admits to having had a platonic relationship with a man younger than she. She has been employed to do household work, though she is not very skilled. Her appetite is capricious (prefers spices, vinegars); she often has nausea, vomiting.

Sensitivity to contact, pinching, tickling. Cold and heat are not perceived except on the left foot and leg and right foot. Tickling is perceptible in the right nostril. Responsiveness is obtuse on the veil of the palate and at the base of the tongue. The mucous membranes of the external auditory ducts, the eyelids, and the eyeballs are nonresponsive. The same is true of the labial mucous membranes. She complains of double vision. This is a point that needs verification.

We ask D. questions. *Do you have any brothers?* I have one. *What were you doing in the region of Dieppe?* My mother wanted me to establish myself as a seamstress.

5 December – Attack of hysteria. Agitation, violent temper. D. bit one of her fellow patients. D. is laid on the floor in order to apply ovarian compression. Pulse: eighty-four. When she returns to herself, D. tells us the attack was preceded by the same phenomenon as previous attacks: She is upset. She has the desire to call out. She feels in her arms and legs the sensation of threads being pulled through. She feels as though she is made of ice.

6 December – Nothing much in particular.

The Bells of Loudun

The birth presented no complications. [Geneviève] wanted to breast-feed but circumstances necessitated placing the infant at the hospice of the rue d'Enfer. She had an abscess of the left breast—the one whose nipple she had previously cut off.

—*Iconographie de la Salpêtrière*, vol. 1, 1877

S TILL, YOU ARE NOT *Abandonée* number 24,641. Since you were born, fifteen years ago, since you were taken from me soon after, and now, and always, you have had a name. There have been times I have wanted to carve it into my arm the way Mother Joan of the Angels carved *Jesus, Mary, Joseph* into hers, but then the carving, too, would become part of the story they tell, another way in which I am like Mother Joan and not myself. The doctors' stories have endings. My stories never finish.

Here is one: Each morning at five o'clock, the grandmother from my second foster family took us to hear the first Mass. It was the only Mass where the priest sang "Pange Lingua" before giving the Holy Sacrament and so, she said, it had greater value for our souls than the other Masses. Afterward, I would go to confession and scrounge up an answer to the priest's question, *What next, my child?* There was a quarter hour to fill and so: gluttony, inattention to my prayers, pilfering. Still, I could not recite the Gospel. The priest would begin, *Jesus said to His disciples . . .* My mind went blank. It went elsewhere. Where did it go? I would like to tell you where my mind went. I want to tell you the parts that have no words.

For example, the doctors always want to know about the pain, how much, and does it hurt. Don't ever tell anyone how much it hurts. When I cut off my nipple, it hurt just enough. *Why?* the doctors asked, then answered it must be related to a fanatical Christian sect from Russia I had never heard of. They castrated their men and amputated the nipples of their women. My answer was half question: *Because I was on fire?* I kept to myself: No demons, no angels, or, rather, when my ecstasy takes me, whether there are or there aren't doesn't matter. It makes me bigger. If it's demons making me less gray and small, so what. Isn't it better to be a hot devil body than to eat beans in oil every day? When you were born, I could not nurse you because of the abscess, but that isn't why they took you away. Don't tell anyone what you really love.

The first time I went in search of you, I was detained by Prussian officers stationed in Burgundy after the armistice. They said you were there, or near there. They said you were with a good family. I don't think they ever knew where you were. Anyway, why would they tell me? Before I was detained, I stumbled into a town with good soil for flax and oats, strong vodka. Only its apple trees gone wrong. The pigs in that town ate well. They were enormous. They didn't mind the sour, sour apples. The nuns ate well, too, all those fat pigs. No wonder they were rumored to dance. Every woman has a natural inclination to fall, they say. Let women suffer, they say; it is their fate. Don't listen to them, though there will be days, weeks, when it will feel true. There were holes in the roof of the inn near the stone convent in that town. The convent was severe in its beauty, clean the way the mind wishes to be. In the court-yard, white habits hung on clotheslines made out of wood poles that creaked in the wind. There were pigeons everywhere. I want to tell you the feeling of coming upon that town. A moment on the way somewhere, sharp with the morning light of possibility. That is the feeling of searching for you. Later, the Prussian officers detained me for long enough that I became pregnant with a second child who did not live. The doctors said the famous Mother Joan of the Angels had convulsions, too, but unlike her, your sister died of them. She was six weeks old. That story does not finish either.

In the story the doctors tell, I am no mother. I am an orphan. I am the first entry of that year in the town registry of Loudun. You began in Loudun, the doctors tell me. You are from the same place as Mother Joan of the Angels. All their stories begin this way. For years, I believed them. Mother Joan, to whom a satanic vision appeared over two hundred years ago in the form of a handsome priest who spent years seducing local widows and unhappy wives. Mother Joan, whom the priests, the unhandsome ones, strapped to a bench, waving wooden crosses in her face; still she threw off the ropes, shouting, I am and I will be. The demons, she told the priests, took the form of a rhinoceros, or a dinosaur, or Leviathan risen from the sea. Eight devils—in this arm and that one, in this leg and that one, lodged in her belly, and between her legs (Dog's Tail, that one was called). Those were the words for what was inside her. If someone had asked why, maybe she would have answered differently. Maybe her answer would have been half question, too: *Because I was on fire?*

Between foster families, I was kept by nuns. The doctors

thought they were bringing me the news of Mother Joan, but it was my own nuns who told me of the nuns under Mother Joan's watch, whose visions took the shape of hers. Because they were on fire? Their minds filled with the handsome priest. They swirled and flirted in their habits, sleeves like wings. All of that fasting and mortification, everyone always lying down on the ground, prostrating themselves. No more, their bodies said, we are through with this world. There is another world and it is in us.

People came to watch them twirl, to watch the priests flick holy water at them, to listen as it sizzled against their hot devil bodies. The nuns growled and sweated and hissed and rolled around on the cold stone floor, my nuns told me. They swirled out of the convent and through the muddy pig troughs after it rained, dirtying their skirts, my nuns would say. Their stories trailed off, a warning and a wish. People love a holy fire. That the devil is here, alongside God, it's how the world likes it.

They say the bells in Loudun toll for lost travelers. I was eight when I escaped from the home of the first foster family. I thought I was lost in the woods, lost in the trees, but I didn't know the half of being lost, or maybe I knew exactly half. If I had known what was to come and what was to go, I'd have walked straight into the shadows cast by the branches of those lost trees. The bells tolled me out of the woods, tolled me out of the shadows. What was I even looking for? Another child in the family, a boy they said was my brother, told me someone left me in a *tour* when I was a baby. I looked for a *tour*, but *tour* turned out not to be a tower at all, but a revolving deposit box built into the side of a church. Because your real parents were too poor, or maybe everyone was dead, said the boy they said was my brother. His parents were only a little poor and not dead. Put the baby in, turn the box, close the door, ring the bell, he'd explained. The lost baby, found again by the nun on the other side. I walked and walked, away from the farm into the woods, wondering, What is it, the distance between lost and found? Every time I look for you, I wonder what is that distance.

Maybe my stories are not stories at all. Here is another: I was fourteen when my suitor died of brain fever. My third set of foster parents forbade me to go the funeral because they never approved, but I wanted to see was he there, was it true. When they took me home, for two days I was like the corpse I never found, but the feeling of him has never been lost to me. It is in me somewhere still.

By the time I was deposited in that box, the government had made the boxes smaller, then smaller still, so only the smallest children would fit. Someone turned that box and, small as I was, I was found again. How could I have ever been lost when I was always in that small, small box? You were always somewhere. You were never lost to me. You are somewhere still.

Here is another: For a time, I hauled coal and wood in the home of a Monsieur L. Because I did not want the baby, I threw myself around the room and hoarded belladonna pills. I was brought to a hospital and kept from dying in order to save the child who never existed. Taken, dead, imagined, the mother part of me is just as gone as all of you. The doctors are not wrong, but what is this fierce attachment? It has no words, and still I want to tell it to you.

There were whispered stories among my nuns: The door handle covered with soot, that's how Mother Joan of the

Angels made the palm print on the white stone she claimed belonged to one of the demons. I don't blame them. When the doctors told me Mother Joan's belly, too, had swelled, that her breasts, too, had dripped with milk, all for a baby who did not exist, I wanted to find the root of her and cut it out. Could I not have a catastrophe that was my own? We are the same, but not in the way the doctors tell it.

The lost travelers for whom the bells toll in Loudun? We were never lost. We were always somewhere with a ringing inside us. We rang ourselves out of the woods, out of the trees. We do not begin and end. We ring and ring and ring. Who needs a story to live?

After she died, they put Mother Joan of the Angels's head in a reliquary. Soon it became clear that visitors came to the church only to see her skull displayed on a silk pillow behind glass. The church officials removed it, buried her bones, and built a crucifix big enough to keep people coming.

I still have a fistful of Loudun dust. I first gathered it up when I was eight because, it is true, I did imagine Mother Joan of the Angels walking the earth centuries ago, her feet touching that dirt. I did feel something for her. I put the dirt in my apron and carried it back to the farm, where, as I suspected, I wouldn't be for much longer. When I turned nine, my family no longer received money for fostering me, and I was sent back to the nuns. I carried the dirt trod long ago by Mother Joan of the Angels in a little pouch, replenished it when I returned to Loudun years later, walked it from Paris to Le Quesnoy, from Le Quesnoy to Bois-d'Haine, walked it all the way to the cottage of the girl stigmatic, where I sprinkled it on her doorstep so all of us might walk the same patch of earth. We are, all of us, you, too, walking the same patch of earth. What I felt for Mother Joan isn't something I can explain, even now. What *did* Jesus say to His disciples? I still don't know. My mind still goes elsewhere. When they took you from me, I had no words. I have no words. This is a pitiful effort at words. Stories always are. Still, you are not *Abandonée* number 24,641. Your name is Desirée, the desired one. Mornings when you lie in wet grass and wonder, Am I myself? It is endless what is inside you.

Whipping Nettles

We can cut them, prick them, and burn them, and they feel nothing. Even better, these completely numb spots are so poorly irrigated that when we would [cut] them, there is not one drop of blood. The hysterics are very proud of their immunity and amuse themselves by passing long needles through their arms and legs.

—Paul Regnard
"L'Anesthésie hystérique" (1887)

Some of us were once devoted to the Sacred Heart. Jesus, not surprisingly, is a jealous lover. Give me your heart, He said, placing it in His own chest; from that ardent oven, He removed a heart-shaped flame and placed it in the heart-shaped space where our hearts used to be, and then we only blazed for Him. In the before, sometimes we were the girl who passed a knotty apple tree every day on her way to work on the farm where she didn't feel the whipping nettles the farmer used when she didn't do her work. That's not true. She felt it. She wanted to feel it.

The color of the era of soul science is the red of our blood and the blood of Christ, which, unlike our own blood, we have not seen. Still, we believe in the blood of Christ, or maybe we used to before we, the unbest girls, lived in the blurry dark of the in-between, neither this nor that. The color of the era of soul science is the red of fury. In the before, sometimes there were days the factory foreman asked the owner for a raise for us and pocketed the difference. There were days there was soup for lunch no dog would eat and we walked back through the doors of the dormitory to sleep on the sack of wood shavings that was our mattress in the attic and we wished the roof tiles so close above our heads would crush the hunger and us along with it.

Sometimes we are the girl who lived on the edge. Thriving or dying, lost or found, appearing or disappearing? The edge does not ask these questions; it is these questions and they are the color red. Maybe the red began long before she was wanted or unwanted, faithful or fallen, counted or unclaimed. The fury, freezing cold at first, not hot as she would have imagined, comes from the earth itself, up through her feet. Everything, her fault. The spilled milk, the stolen currants, the torn linens, the smashed plates. Pull the bones out of herself, smash it all, press the tiny shards of glass hard into her skin until they are as lost as she is, for weeks, for years, forever. She beats everyone—madame, monsieur, the doctors, herself—senseless with her thighbone. Bone against bone. Is she real now? How about now?

The fury began before she was old enough to give it a name. When she arrived at the hospital, dragged through the door into the red era of soul science, her fury was called hysteria, as if it had nothing to do with her, and she became we. and we became the disease that said we wanted to steal, to falsely accuse, to set things on fire. Fine, let it burn.

Case Notes (1889)

2 June – General rigidity. Amyl nitrate. Attacks suspended; at three o'clock, a crisis, then nothing. Evening temperature: thirty-eight degrees.

3 June – No attacks since yesterday. Deafness on both sides; stronger on the left. Itching. Retention of urine for five or six days; a liter of urine by catheter. Constipation. Any trace of contracture has disappeared. Menstruation began this morning.

4 June – V. does not eat. Deafness and retention of urine persist. Evening temperature: thirty-eight degrees.

5 June – Morning and evening temperature: thirty-eight degrees.

6 June – The patient has more or less returned to her normal state.

24 July – V., who had not had any crises since June 2, resumed having attacks yesterday at four o'clock. Evening temperature: 38.6 degrees. This morning, the attacks continue. Morning temperature: 38.2 degrees. In the intervals between attacks, tetanic state with contractures of the jaws, ulcer of the lips (patient bit herself). Clonic state. Rhythmic jerking more pronounced—trunk flails violently. The attacks end four o'clock. Evening temperature: thirty-eight degrees.

25 July – V. has not slept. Deafness gone. Series of seizures; eyes rolled back in her head. She shouts, "Oh, oh, oh!" Repeats five or six times, intervals ten minutes each. No laughter, no tears. V. says she has a beast in her stomach. Chats incessantly, a veritable delusion of words. *Count on me: you have my friendship. . . . You told me that you would cure me. . . . I swear I did not say anything to the doctors.* (She appears to be conversing with a lover, reassuring him about the police.) *Surely two months without having seizures, and I get out. Emile, you're not nice, dirty pig! Oh, how to trust men! Oh! The peacocks and their tails!*

A Heartless Child

OUR HANDS IN THE ROOM DUCHENNE, the room Bouvier, the room Requin; our legs in the room Leguin, the room Rayer, the passage Lepic; our heads in the room Cruvellier and the room Pruss; our bodies on a platform like a stage set in rooms who knows where or which. In the hospital, there were endless photographs of us. The photographs taken when we first arrived (here is someone) were different from the ones taken ever after (here, what she became). The ever-after photographs of the doctor's best girls making shapes that spell hysteria (*arc en cercle* or some other grand movement, ecstasy or some other passionate attitude) were hung in the hospital corridors, in the passageways that led to the photography annex, to the school, where we learned grammar, history, geography, and sums, to the gymnasium, where we learned to bend and not to break, and to the library, where those of us who were able to read borrowed books, and in the amphitheater, where those best girls made the shapes, and in the offices of the doctors who taught the best girls how to make the shapes. In the photographs taken when we first arrived, we did not yet know how to write the illness with the jumble of our bodies. Some of us never learned.

In the photographs taken when we first arrived: a fist punches out of a frayed cuff, a thumb extended, wrinkles underlining the knuckle; a hand rests on a cloth-draped cone;

a set of legs dangle from a table, one foot bent at a peculiar angle; a body in profile, its arm twisted behind its back, the spine's knobby staircase, upon which rests the hand of a doctor. Around his wrist, a watch frozen in its ticking.

A card accompanied each intake photograph. Voucher for the photograph of Mademoiselle such and such. Room: Duchenne, Bouvier, Requin, Leguin, Rayer, etc. Diagnosis: Hysteria, Paralysis of the face or eyes or feet, etc., or Hysteria, atrophy of the tongue or hands or hips, etc., or Hysteria, hysterical yawning or crying or laughing, etc., or Hysteria, contracture of the legs or foot or abdominal muscles, etc.

Sometimes there was a card and the photograph was me. *M. Dubois, 12 August 1890, age 20. Room: Leguin. Diagnosis: Hysteria, contracture of the hand. Information: Present for six months. Occurred following a violent emotion.* My hair, an electric frizz above my high-necked blouse. Beads for eyes, a flat mouth. A tag dangling from my wrist, my hand curled, stiff, propped up on the back of a chair.

My loneliness, my shadow. The past takes the shape of clothes too heavy for a clothesline. The wet weight of them pulls me back. Sometimes at Monsieur B.'s, for example, I didn't wring the clothes enough after washing them. Too heavy for the clothesline strung across the large kitchen garden, they fell into the dirt, into the carrot greens and lettuce. I would have to start over. Mornings, I eyed the basin for washing vegetables, just big enough to drown myself. It would have been difficult; still, I thought, I could fall in, make it so people would think it was an accident. You cannot imagine the kind of sadness that enters the heart of a girl. Fifteen pretending to be nineteen, the age my parents gave the woman of the house so she would hire me. She wanted someone older (*mature* was the word she used, by which she meant a lot of things, none of them fifteen and beautiful).

In the garden was a large plot of red currants. We who worked in the house were given permission to eat as many as we liked once they were ripe. Somehow, they were never quite ripe. There would be an occasional announcement: The currants are ripe, ripe enough for preserves; then another: Oh no, no wait, not yet. I began to feel about the currants the way I felt then about my body—curious, imaginative, eager, greedy. Everything made me want to touch myself. I wanted to rub the currants all over myself. I walked around filled with an aching anger. One night, another announcement—No, no wait, not yet—and I couldn't stand it anymore. I decided to wake up early and eat as many of the ruby red bunches as I could. In the early morning, I sneaked out into the garden. At first, I gathered the sweet fruit in my apron; soon I was eating them straight off the bush.

I returned to the kitchen, sick with fruit, and there was Monsieur B. Help yourself, he said. He had been watching from the window. The kitchen shutters I thought I had shut? Juice on my lips and I had not shut them.

You don't look nineteen, he said. He stepped closer.

Did he want me to look nineteen or fifteen? I knew right then I looked exactly the way he wanted me to look, that I wanted to make money to buy underwear enough so I could change it several times a week and still have money to send home, that to say nothing was to say something. I smiled a smile borrowed from who knows where, some catalog of smiles designed to ruin a man.

I am the right age, I said.

Heartless girl, he said. He stepped closer still, licked the juice from my lips. My lie, my secrets, just as delicious, making of me a mystery. Some men love to jump right into that gap. The currants gathered in my apron? I smashed them on my face, my neck. The juice dripped down.

Here, I said. Angry, aching, I offered him my throat.

Every morning, I went into the garden early. Every morning, I left the kitchen shutters open. The red currants made me just sick enough. For a while, that sickness was what I wanted. There was so much juice for him to lick. I bought new underwear. I sent money home. I knew, the way I knew what to say that first day in the kitchen, the way I knew what to do after, he would tire of me. Soon his wife understood and hired a more mature girl.

I left the country for the city. There was plenty of work there, I'd heard. Mounting the eyes and beaks of birds onto hats, stringing pearls and spangles on fancy braid work, the cost of the braid deducted from your pay, still, it could be enough for a while. There was the stitching to be done that held in place the whalebone stays of corsets. I found an apartment above a hardware store, where all day long I listened to talk of nails and cookware. An attic apartment, its poorly joined planks creaked when I walked on them, whistled my name when the wind blew through.

I found work in a dressmaker's firm. I got up early to go to work and went to bed late (the thing about sewing was you could take it home). I got up early, went to bed late, woke up a girl who believed that sewing mended something. I got up early, went to bed late, got up early, went to bed late, woke up wondering, Mended what?

One day I woke up a woman who received a steamer trunk sent by her sister. The woman I had become had no more dresses, and so my sister sent her castoffs. I needed them, but I wanted not a single one of them. I wanted the finely embroidered dresses I made, the silk dresses spun from the *tavelles*. I wanted a dress with fringe. A dress with fur trim. I wanted ankle boots. I wanted hats decorated with the eyes and beaks of birds, with strung pearls and spangles and fancy braid work. Why wouldn't sewing luxury items eleven hours a day give me a taste for finery. Leave off the question mark, its pleading curve. I am tired of begging.

Some months before, I had written:

Dear Mother, May I keep the six francs that is our raise? I will still send the same amount of my salary home, don't worry.

Not: I rise at four, sew until eight, dress myself in order to arrive at the workshop by eight-thirty, stay until nine, come home for dinner, work until midnight. Not: I skip the midday meal in order to save for one of the dresses I make.

Folded in among the ratty dresses in the trunk was a note from my mother, meant not for me but for my sister.

My dear little girl, you're just like me: a generous nature, unlike your sister. She hangs on to her money. She is a heartless child.

There have been moments I have wondered did my jealous sister send the letter on purpose. Before I received the steamer trunk, I had no doubt there was love for me in this world. I have never thought myself extraordinary, but love, no matter the circumstances, it is. After the trunk, after the letter, all I could think was, In this steaming hell I will remain unknown. Even my heartlessness will remain unknown except, maybe, to those who no longer love me. I opened the trunk and there I was, a heartless girl after all.

Otherwise, years passed in which I did not throw myself

out the window. Then a man I sometimes saw in the evening took me to see *Carmen* at the Opéra-Comique. Michaela sang to Don José his mother's message: *Tell him his mother / thinks of him night and day; / that she misses him and that she hopes / that she forgives and that she waits.* Art worked the way it should: It was a message from my own mother.

I saved for a year in order to return to her. Did I think I would prove I was not heartless? I bought some fabric and stole the rest in order to make a dress not for me but for her, a dress made by a Parisian seamstress, me. My loneliness. My shadow. Brilliant green silk, fringed, fur-trimmed. I would alter it to fit once I was there with her, back in my village. I would lay hands on her body, that body in whose parentheses I first existed, now a stranger's. I unreeled—not breaking not breaking not breaking—the skeins of silk. When I was done, I wrapped the dress in crinkling brown paper, held it in my lap on the long ride home, the sound of the *tavelles* still in my head, louder than the train.

It was evening when I arrived in Dauphine. The sun, which flooded the valley of the Cévennes during the day, was a wave of light receding. The end of the workday: Men rubbed down the sweaty horses; women set enormous pots of soup on long outdoor tables. All as I had left it fifteen years before, I thought. This is what heartless daughters think, as if the world were a stage and they the heroines of their lives and everyone else's, too. I wished I was the girl who sat beside me in the dress workshop, her sewing fervor verging on religion. She rose at four, sewed until eight, dressed herself in order to arrive at the workshop by eight thirty, where she stayed until nine, went home for dinner, worked until midnight, and skipped the midday meal not in order to buy a beautiful dress, but to one day return to a place in the country like this one, where she might have a house with a garden and chicken and rabbits. She didn't want to go hungry in old age the way she had as a child, to starve to death in a city still strange after so many years. She wanted to live in a village like mine, where the sun set behind the Cévennes and people called to one another as they left the vineyards for the day in a local dialect I couldn't understand from having been away so long.

There was a man brushing his boots off outside the house I had decided was mine out of all of the other look-alike houses. What is it, madame? he said. What startled me most was that I could understand him.

The brown package with its secret dress was still clutched to my chest—had I set it down even once the entire ride? I'm fine, thank you, I began to say, and then the man was my father.

I am your daughter, I said, something as simple and stupid as that. Still he went on not recognizing me, asserting his confusion with an expression borrowed from a novel he would never read, in which a man does not recognize his daughter, a look that said the bond of blood relatedness is not a forever bond. It was a look that feared requests for money.

Is Mother home? I asked.

Who is your mother?

I have something for her, I said, and held up the package.

I have something for her, too, that impossible woman!

He forgot what he had forgotten.

She was alive. That would have been enough. I didn't need what happened next. I still don't. The door of the familiar house opened and she peered out, that woman who was my mother. She saw me and closed the door again. Once my mother; now, and forever, a woman closing the door.

Impossible, the man who was my father said under his breath.

I thought about giving the dress to the girl sewing her way fervently back to the country, but she dreamed of chickens and rabbits, not a green silk dress. I left the package in a train station in a town outside of Paris, where it might be discovered by someone as heartless as me.

I rose at four, sewed until eight, dressed myself in order to arrive at the workshop by eight thirty, stayed until nine at night, came home for dinner, worked until midnight. I did not skip the midday meal. I got up early, went to bed late, got up early, went to bed late. Time passed like this until I woke up one day and began to write a letter to that woman, now and forever closing the door.

> *Dear mother,*
>
> *How are you? I am sewing with a religious fervor in order to one day return home, to have a house in the country with a garden and chicken and rabbits. To return to the village with the sun setting behind the Cévennes, to hear people calling to one another as they leave the vineyards for the day in the language I was born speaking. I am sewing my way into a peaceful garden with flowers.*

I tried again.

> *Dear mother,*
>
> *How are you? I am fervently sewing my way back to you.*

It is exhausting how much of life is spent trying to say what you mean. Too many words, too few, all that feeble punctuation.

Dear mother,

The words kept disappearing, until one day there were no more.

Did the girl dream of sewing her way back to the country-side because the countryside she dreamed of was not dreaming of her? Did Don José's mother forgive him precisely because he would never return? Is the better part of life in the missing? On the train ride back from my village, after I was free of the package, what I wanted most of all was to become imaginary, so that I might be forgiven. In this, I have succeeded.

In the room Cruvellier, a face in profile, the whorl of an ear, a curl escaped from a knot of hair; in the passage Lepic, a set of legs hang off a table, bloomers pushed up to reveal a shin, at the bottom of which, a foot, toes curled; in some room somewhere, some body collapsing, held up by a nurse— she has turned to smile for the camera; in a room somewhere else, some body walking away, naked except for boots, dimples above her ass; in the room Leguin, a hand, stiff on a table, veins crisscrossing the back of it. Blood pumped through. It pumped through. It pumps through.

Bodies, We Are in Them

Or MAYBE, IN THE BEFORE, we lived by the coast and swam in the sounding sea.

We swam in the sea and there were rocks underfoot and birds overhead. These bodies, we were in them, and they were in the sea. There were days, seconds, when the difference between these bodies and the sea went away. The light on the water and the wave and the next wave always coming. When we staggered out of the waves, the sand sucked at our ankles, sucking us down. The water didn't want to leave us. Its salt clings to us still.

Sometimes a door swings open, and an *I* breaks free, an *I* who walked in the night from the factory to the dormitory where she once lived, an *I* so small before the moon, while in the forest the trees grow bigger. The moon grows, too. I am small, but I make enormous soul-size shadows on the road. *Her loneliness, her shadow.* Here in the blurry dark, I take shape. I return—*my loneliness, my shadow.* Then I am gone, same as those from the before who may or may not still be living in the world of regular days—mother, father, sister, brother, Delphine, Bardella, Louise, Sarina. They appear in our dreams, and how are they not here with us in the smell of damp stone and near bodies? We wake up and of course they are not here, but we are.

The cypress trees reached toward the sun, branches bending and dividing, as joyous as we were at being in the water, at becoming light flashing on its surface. No, even then, we knew it was not joy the trees felt. It was something better. To be a tree was to be without the burden of joy, which gives way eventually, we would learn soon enough, to nostalgia. To be a tree, to lean in the direction of the sun! Not in order to forget, but because that is simply what you are meant to do. In the winter, the world shrank to a cold dot of light; the stripped tree branches carved lines into the sky as full of yearning as when they leaned into the summer sun, but not yearning at all. We will never understand. Whatever season, nature goes about its business when we aren't looking; its magnificence doesn't need us to look.

Giant blue agaves grow by the sea, their spines sharp and cutting. A line sliced across our arm when we brushed past on the way down to the water, like the doctors' knives spelling the name of the disease on our bodies, but the agave wasn't trying to spell anything. The sea washed away the blood, its salt healed the wound, but the scar is there still. Some days it reminds us of the agave's enormous flower shooting up to bloom exactly once, its desiccated skeleton haunting the earth for months and then crumbling. Some days it reminds us every beginning contains its end.

My loneliness, my shadow, and I swim in the sea on an ordinary day, salt on my skin, the sunlight ricocheting off the water, a rock underfoot, a bird overhead. My body, I am in it, and it is in the sea. The light on the water, the light on the water, the light on the water. The wave and the wave and the next wave always coming. I trace the rough design of the bark of the cypress tree going about its business; it maps the vast geography of the rest of my life. I will go there and there and there. I try to be light I try to be water I try to be bird, but I am a body here where there are no ordinary days, here where, most days, there are no days at all.

The before, the just before, and the centuries of just befores. A door swings open. We were saints. We were witches. We were burned at the stake. We are on fire still.

Notes and Credits

Page 11: *The spells and lethargic states? I could not do otherwise. Besides, it was not a bit of fun. Simulation? Lots of fakes tried; the great doctor gave them one look and said, Be still.* This is derived from an alleged quote from Blanche Wittmann in *Charcot, The Clinician: The Tuesday Lessons: Excerpts from Nine Case Presentations on General Neurology Delivered at the Salpêtrière Hospital in 1887–88*, by Jean-Martin Charcot, translated by Christopher G. Goetz.

Pages 12, 13, and 14—photo credits:
Façade principal des divisions Mazarin, Lassay, de la chapelle et des jardins (s.d.). Archives de l'Assistance Publique—Hôpitaux de Paris, 3Fi4-Pitié-Salpêtrière-1366.

Chapelle Saint-Louis depuis l'allée avec des patients (1910). Archives de l'Assistance Publique—Hôpitaux de Paris, 3Fi4-Pitié-Salpêtrière-0124.

Façade de l'entreé avec la statue de Charcot en place (s.d.). Archives de l'Assistance Publique—Hôpitaux de Paris, 3Fi4-Pitié-Salpêtrière-1358.

Page 22: At the Salpêtrière, photographic cards were used to catalog incoming patients. The photographic cards throughout the book are inventions based on the Salpêtrière's model form found in Georges Didi-Huberman's *The Invention of Hysteria*.

Page 23: From *La Révolution surréaliste*, vol. 11 (1928). From gallica.bnf.fr/Bibliothèque nationale de France.

In the eleventh issue of *La Révolution surréaliste* (March 1928), André Breton and Louis Aragon published a manifesto on the fiftieth anniversary of the diagnosis of hysteria, accompanied by photographs taken at the Salpêtrière of Jean-Martin Charcot's patient Augustine.

Page 31: *Iconographie photographique de la Salpêtrière* is the three-volume medical reference book—case histories, photographs, illustrations—produced by students of the neurologist Jean-Marie Charcot, Désiré-Magloire Bourneville and Paul-Marie-Léon Régnard, and published by Bureaux du Progrès Médical (Bureau of Medical Progress) between 1876 and 1880. This page—and all of the case notes and illustrations (pages 41 and 69) throughout the book—is part invention, part rough translation of a page from *Iconographie photographique de la Salpêtrière*.

Page 40: Ernest Mesnet, Fig. 3, *Autographisme et Stigmates, Revue de l'hypnotisme et de la psychologie physiologique*, vol. 4 (1890). From the collection of the New York Public Library.

Page 46: Ernest Mesnet, Fig. 1, *Autographisme et Stigmates*. From *Nervosisme: Autographisme et stigmates dans la sorcellerie au XVIe siècle*, by Ernest Mesnet. From the collection of the Bibliothèque interuniversitaire de Santé, Université de Paris.

Page 51: *Debut de L'Attaque.* Photograph of Geneviève Basile Legrand by Paul Regnard from Désiré-Magloire Bourneville and Paul-Marie-Léon Regnard, *Iconographie photographique de la Salpêtrière,* vol. 1 (Paris: Aux Bureaux de Progrès Médical, Delahaye & Lecrosnier, 1877), Plate 15. Medical Historical Library, Harvey Cushing/John Hay Whitney Medical Library, Yale University.

Page 53: *Terminal Period: Ecstasy.* Photograph of Geneviève Basile Legrand by Paul Regnard from Désiré-Magloire Bourneville and Paul-Marie-Léon Regnard, *Iconographie photographique de la Salpêtrière,* vol. 1 (Paris: Aux Bureaux de Progrès Médical, Delahaye & Lecrosnier, 1877), Plate 24. Medical Historical Library, Harvey Cushing/John Hay Whitney Medical Library, Yale University.

Page 57: *Hystero-Epilepsy: Succubus.* Photograph of Geneviève Basile Legrand by Paul Regnard from Désiré-Magloire Bourneville and Paul-Marie-Léon Regnard, *Iconographie photographique de la Salpêtrière,* vol. 2 (Paris: Aux Bureaux de Progrès Médical, Delahaye & Lecrosnier, 1877), Plate 39. Medical Historical Library, Harvey Cushing/John Hay Whitney Medical Library, Yale University.

Page 59: The obituary of Louise Lateau, a mystic and a stigmatic, first appeared in *London Truth,* reprinted in *The New York Times,* September 8, 1883.

Page 60: From a letter dated August 12, 1876, from Dr. Decaesseckey of Quesnoy-sur-Deuele to Dr. Jean-Martin Charcot of Paris, as translated by Asti Hustvedt in *Medical Muses: Hysteria in Nineteenth-Century Paris* (W. W. Norton, 2011).

Page 71: These are the last lines of "Le Foi qui Guerit" ("The Faith That Cures," 1892), Jean-Martin Charcot's last published article.

image: *Une leçon clinique à la Salpêtrière*, by André Brouillet. Université Paris Descartes; photograph from Wikimedia Commons.

An engraving of this painting hung over Sigmund Freud's couch in his London office. The painting depicts one of Charcot's weekly public demonstrations, known as the Tuesday Lessons, in which he described neurological case studies, including hysteria, using patients as live models. Anna Freud wrote of the image, "It held a strange attraction for me in my childhood, and I often asked my father what was wrong with the patient. The answer I always got was that she was 'too tightly laced.'"

Page 85: These case notes are from *Iconographie photographique de la Salpêtrière*, vol. 3, p. 19, as translated by Asti Hustvedt in *Medical Muses: Hysteria in Nineteenth-Century Paris*.

Page 86: *Leçons cliniques sur l'hystérie et l'hypnotisme faites à l'Hôpital Saint-André de Bordeaux*, by Albert Pitres (1891). Scanned by Francis A. Countway Library, Harvard University.

Page 89: Photograph of Jane Avril, by Paul Sescau. From Biblioteca Nacional de Espana.

Page 118: *Pinel Freeing the Insane* (1876). Photogravure by Goupil, after painting by Tony Robert-Fleury. From the Collection of the United States National Library of Medicine.

Story Credits:

The following stories were previously published in slightly different form: "The City Itself" in *The New England Review*; "Twenty Thousand Leagues Under the Sea" in *The American Scholar*; "The Inclination to Believe" and "Her Godly Imagination" as "Two Inclinations" in *Conjunctions*; "Father, Ether, Sea" in *Conjunctions*; "Never the Same Way Twice" in *AGNI*; "The Bells of Loudun" in *Bennington Review*; "A Heartless Child," in *Five Points: A Journal of Literature & Art.* "In the Before," "The Dull Stage of Reality," "Time's Signature," "Whipping Nettles," and "Bodies, We Are in Them," were published together, in slightly different form, as "A Door Swings Open" in *The Georgia Review*.

Acknowledgments

City of Incurable Women owes a debt of gratitude to cities of other books, cities of other people; to list them all would require another city altogether. Thank you, in particular, to Asti Hustvedt's *Medical Muses: Hysteria in Nineteenth-Century Paris* and Georges Didi-Huberman's *Invention of Hysteria: Charcot and the Photographic Iconography of the Salpêtrière.* Thank you to Laura Larson for our bountiful collaboration and for your friendship, and to Amy Yoes for making the connection. Thank you to the editors of the publications in which these stories first appeared: *AGNI, The American Scholar, Bennington Review, Conjunctions, Five Points, The Georgia Review, New England Review.* Thank you to the magnificent Alice Tasman. Thank you to Erika Goldman for her vision, and to Carol Edwards, Joe Gannon, Laura Hart, and everyone at Bellevue Literary Press.

For the gift of space and time, my thanks to the Bogliasco Foundation, the Brown Foundation Fellows Program at the Dora Maar House, the John Simon Guggenheim Foundation, MacDowell, and the University of Maryland Graduate School. For the gift of beautiful places in which to write and wander, my thanks to Adobe Chi and Stewart Parker. For the gift of Patuxent Research Refuge, my thanks to Nicolette Polek.

Thank you to generous readers and dear friends. In particular, Lindsay Bernal, Chris Bohner, Gedalya Chinn, Stacey D'Erasmo, Julia Greenberg, Emily Mitchell, Melissa Pritchard, Jessie van Eerden.

Thank you to Emma Parker for archival work that yielded treasures.

And to Michael Parker: abiding love, and thank you.

Bellevue Literary Press is devoted to publishing
literary fiction and nonfiction at the intersection
of the arts and sciences because we believe that
science and the humanities are natural companions
for understanding the human experience.
We feature exceptional literature that explores
the nature of perception and the underpinnings
of the social contract. With each book we publish,
our goal is to foster a rich, interdisciplinary dialogue
that will forge new tools for thinking
and engaging with the world.

To support our press and its mission,
and for our full catalogue of published titles,
please visit us at blpress.org.

BELLEVUE LITERARY PRESS
New York